First published in Great Britain in 2010 by
Random House Books
Random House, 20 Vauxhall Bridge Road,
London SW1V 2SA

www.rbooks.co.uk

The Random House Group Limited Reg. No. 954009

ISBN : 9780099544234

2 4 6 8 10 9 7 5 3 1

Design: Dynamo Limited
Text: Kay Wilkins
Interior Artwork: Ailin Chambers

For information regarding permission,
write to VP Intellectual Property, Ripley Entertainment Inc.,
Suite 188, 7576 Kingspointe Parkway, Orlando, Florida 32819

Email: publishing@ripleys.com
www.ripleysrbi.com

Printed and bound in Great Britain by CPI Bookmarque, Croydon

The Random House Group Limited supports The Forest Stewardship
Council (FSC), the leading international forest certification organisation.
All our titles that are printed on Greenpeace approved FSC certified paper
carry the FSC logo. Our paper procurement policy can be found at:
www.rbooks.co.uk/environment

WINGS
OF FEAR

PUBLISHING

a Jim Pattison Company

Hidden away on a small island off the East Coast of the United States is Ripley High – a unique school for children who possess extraordinary talents.

Located in the former home of Robert Ripley – creator of the world-famous Ripley's Believe It or Not! – the school takes students who all share a secret. Although they look like you or me, they have amazing skills: the ability to conduct electricity, superhuman strength, or control over the weather – these are just a few of the talents the Ripley High School students possess.

The very best of these talented kids have been invited to join a top secret agency – Ripley's Bureau of Investigation: the RBI. This elite group operates from a hi-tech underground base hidden deep beneath the school. From here, the talented teen agents are sent on dangerous missions around the world, investigating sightings of fantastical creatures and strange occurrences. Join them on their incredible adventures as they seek out the weird and the wonderful, and try to separate fact from fiction ...

INTRODUCING THE RBI

The Department of Unbelievable Lies

A mysterious rival agency determined to stop the RBI and discredit Ripley's by sabotaging the Ripley's database

RIPLEY

The spirit of Robert Ripley lives on in RIPLEY, a supercomputer that stores the database – all Ripley's bizarre collections, and information on all the artefacts and amazing discoveries made by the RBI. Featuring a fully interactive holographic Ripley as its interface, RIPLEY gives the agents info on their missions and sends them invaluable data on their R-phones.

THE TEACHERS

Mr Cain

The agents' favourite teacher, Mr Cain, runs the RBI – under the guise of a Museum Club – and coordinates all the agents' missions.

Dr Maxwell

The only other teacher at the school who knows about the RBI, Dr Maxwell equips the agents for their missions with cutting-edge gadgets from his lab.

MEET THE RBI TEAM

As well as having amazing talents, each of the seven members of the RBI has expert knowledge in their own individual fields of interest. All with different skills, the team supports each other at school and while out on missions, where the three most suitable agents are chosen for each case.

The RBI team keep in touch with each other, while on missions, using their R-phones. They also receive facts and useful information from RIPLEY in this way.

▶▶ KOBE

NAME : Kobe Shakur

AGE : 15

SKILLS : Excellent tracking and endurance skills, tribal knowledge and telepathic abilities

NOTES : Kobe's parents grew up in different African tribes. Kobe has amazing tracking capabilities and is an expert on native cultures across the world. He can also tell the entire history of a person or object just by touching it.

▶▶ ZIA

NAME : Zia Mendoza

AGE : 13

SKILLS : Possesses magnetic and electrical powers. Can predict the weather

NOTES : The only survivor of a tropical storm that destroyed her village when she was a baby, Zia doesn't yet fully understand her abilities but she can predict and sometimes control the weather. Her presence can also affect electrical equipment.

▶▶ MAX

NAME : Max Johnson

AGE : 14

SKILLS : Computer genius and inventor

NOTES : Max, from Las Vegas, loves computer games and anything electrical. He spends most of his spare time inventing robots. Max hates school but he loves spending time helping Dr Maxwell come up with new gadgets.

▶▶ KATE

NAME : Kate Jones

AGE : 14

SKILLS : Computer-like memory, extremely clever and ability to master languages in minutes

NOTES : Raised at Oxford University in England by her history professor and part-time archaeologist uncle, Kate memorised every book in the University library after reading them only once!

▶▶ ALEK

NAME : Alek Filipov

AGE : 15

SKILL : Contortionist with amazing physical strength

NOTES : Alek is a member of the Russian under-16 Olympic gymnastics team and loves sports and competitions. He is much bigger than the other agents, and although he seems quiet and serious much of the time, he has a wicked sense of humour.

▶▶ LI

NAME : Li Yong

AGE : 15

SKILL : Musical genius
with pitch-perfect hearing
and the ability to mimic
any sound

NOTES : Li grew up in a
wealthy family in Beijing,
China, and joined Ripley High
later than the other RBI
agents. She has a highly
developed sense of hearing
and can imitate any sound
she hears.

▶▶ JACK

NAME : Jack Stevens

AGE : 14

SKILLS : Can 'talk' to
animals and has expert
survival skills

NOTES : Jack grew up
on an animal park in the
Australian outback. He
has always shared a
strong bond with animals
and can communicate
with any creature –
and loves to eat weird food!

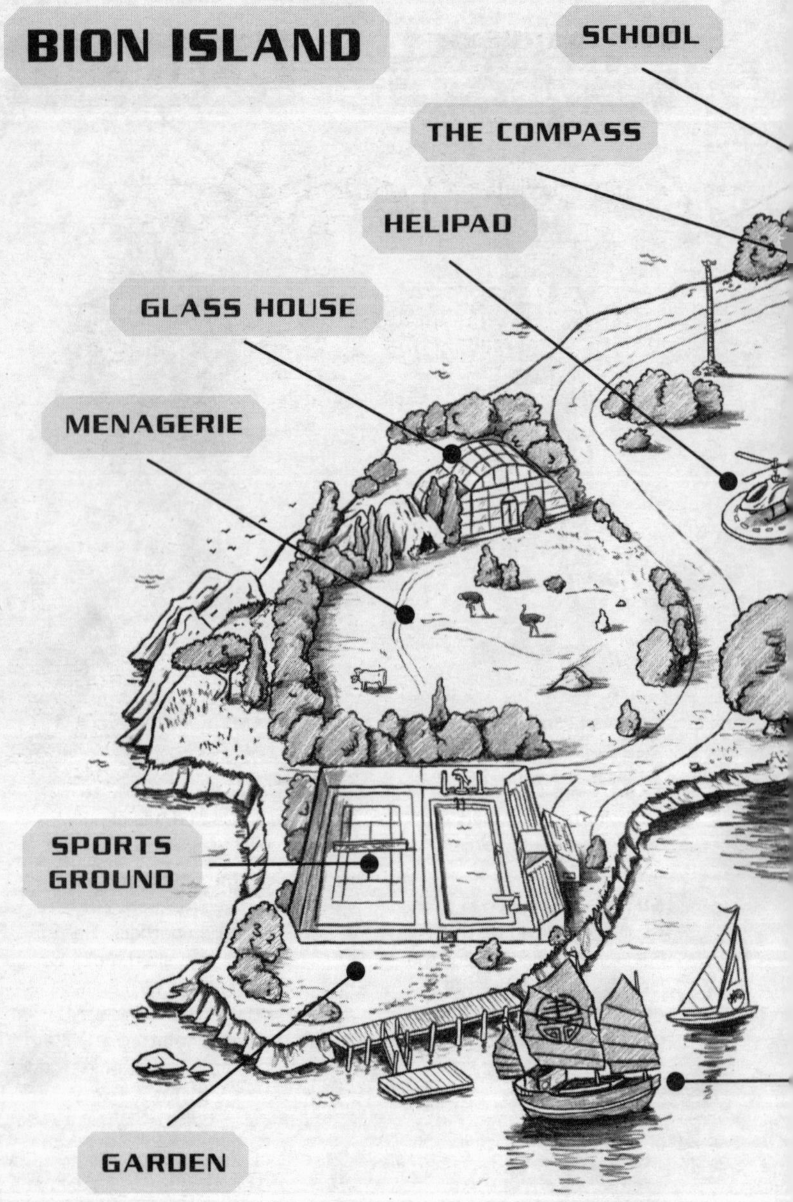

BION ISLAND

SCHOOL

THE COMPASS

HELIPAD

GLASS HOUSE

MENAGERIE

SPORTS GROUND

GARDEN

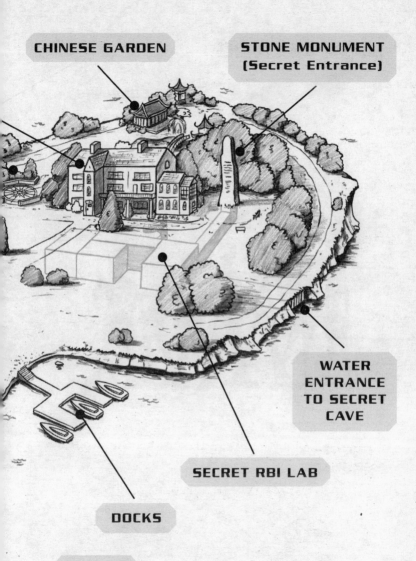

CHINESE GARDEN

STONE MONUMENT
(Secret Entrance)

WATER
ENTRANCE
TO SECRET
CAVE

SECRET RBI LAB

DOCKS

MON LEI

Prologue

It was almost 9:30 and Abby was going to be late for work – again! She rushed out of the underground station, taking the steps up to street level two at a time. Abby had tried so hard to be on time, but last night she had had dinner with her best friend Clare, who she hadn't seen for ages, and they had talked for hours. Then, when her alarm went off this morning, she had just been *so* tired!

As she rushed along the pavement, Abby tried to work out how she was going to get everything done before the Ripley's museum, where she worked, opened – in half an hour.

Suddenly, Abby heard a strange noise. She pulled her phone out of her pocket to see if someone was calling. It wasn't the noise her phone normally made, but it would be just like Clare to have changed the ringtone while she wasn't looking. But the noise wasn't her phone. It grew louder and louder – a high-pitched whine, like an airplane makes just before its engines kick in. Abby looked up to see if there was a plane in trouble, shielding her eyes from the morning sun. As she did so, a large shadow appeared. Huge wings blocked out the sun, and warmth like a fire swallowed up the cool morning breeze. Bright flames lit up the sky as a large flying creature shot past above Abby's head.

Thinking quickly, she switched her phone

to camera mode and tried to get some film of the strange thing. Nobody would believe her about this unless they saw it! Running down the street she filmed until the *thing*, whatever it was, disappeared from view.

Replaying the video Abby looked closely at the screen. It almost seemed as if the creature was surrounded by fire. Abby felt herself go cold with fear. What could it possibly have been?

Closing her phone, Abby ran the rest of the way to work – terrified that the creature might return.

1

Kismet

"I just find it so peaceful here," said Jack. He and Zia were in the Ripley High menagerie. This was home to all the unbelievable animals that Robert Ripley had found on his travels, along with all those that the RBI had discovered on their missions.

Zia listened to the orchestra of animal noises – bird song, monkey calls and barking dogs – and wondered how Jack could think that it was peaceful.

"It's a little bit cold this morning," said Zia, as she pulled her jacket tighter around her.

"It reminds me of home," said Jack, and then Zia understood. He had grown up on an animal park in Australia, so all sorts of weird and wonderful animal noises would have surrounded him there. "Apart from the cold that is!" he added.

Jack was feeding the monkey-pig – a pig with the face of a monkey – and Zia was amazed at how gentle and caring he was with the animals. Just then, there was a blur of fur as something whizzed past them.

▶▶ A piglet born in China in 2008 had the face of a monkey. The newborn had two thin lips, a small nose, two big eyes and its rear legs were considerably longer than its front ones. The shocked owner said that his son likes to play with the creature.

"Oh no, that was Kismet," Zia shrieked.

Kismet, the winged cat, was Zia's favourite animal in the menagerie. Whenever she came with Jack to see the animals, she always made sure that she spent some time with the little creature. She ran off after her and found Buster, the two-nosed dog, sitting at the bottom of one of the trees, looking up expectantly and barking.

"Bad Buster," scolded Zia, as she looked up into the branches to see the multicoloured face of Kismet peering down at her. Carefully, she climbed into the lower part of the tree and picked up the small cat.

"You're shaking," she said, as she put Kismet inside her jacket, partly to keep her warm and partly to protect her while she climbed back down.

▶▶ A cat in China has grown wings. Granny Feng of Xianyang City was amazed to see what started out as two bumps on her cat's back grow into 10-centimetre furry sprouts, like wings, in less than a month in 2007. The wings are likely to have been caused by abnormalities in the cat's genetic make up.

"It's too cold for Kissy here," Zia told Jack when he caught up with her. "And Buster is always tormenting her."

"He can't help it," said Jack, as he scratched the dog's head, both its noses twitching excitedly. "It's what dogs do. And Buster here just has a talent for sniffing out trouble."

"Maybe Kismet could live in my dorm room," suggested Zia. "You'd like that wouldn't you, Kissy?"

The small cat purred from inside Zia's jacket as she tickled its face.

"I bet Mr Clarkson would like that too," Jack said sarcastically. Mr Clarkson was the school caretaker and he was very strict about anything that could make a mess of his beautiful showcase – Ripley High. "Cats in dorm rooms are most definitely 'bad show'." Jack tried to mimic Mr Clarkson's British accent as he delivered the caretaker's catchphrase.

"You're not bad show, are you?" Zia asked the cat. "Pff, what's that?" She waved a hand in front of her face as something flew straight at her head. "It won't leave me alone!" She started to run in circles as the flying thing kept up with her.

"Stay still," suggested Jack. "It's some sort of fly."

"A really annoying one," Zia told him. She zipped her jacket higher to protect Kismet, who was still tucked inside.

"I'll get it," Jack offered, trying to catch the insect that cleverly kept avoiding his grasp. He stopped, thinking he heard laughter, and raised his hand to silence Zia, but she was still trying to lose the fly.

"Ha-ha-ha, something 'bugging' you, Z?" Max stepped out from behind a tree, his face crinkled with laughter.

"Is that fly something to do with you?" Jack asked.

"Maybe ..." Max replied with a wry smile, holding what looked suspiciously like a remote control in his hand.

▶▶ Scientists at Harvard University have created a life-size robotic fly. Weighing only 60 milligrams with a wingspan of just over 2.5 centimetres, it is hoped that the mechanical insects might one day be used as spies or for detecting dangerous chemicals.

▶▶ The US military have developed a way to manipulate real flying beetles using wireless control.

"I should have known," said Jack, not sure if he should be frustrated with Max or impressed by him.

"I told you it was something annoying," said Zia.

"Why don't you direct it away from Zia?" asked Jack.

"It's a robotic homing fly," Max explained. "I set it to track you, Jack, but as always, when something electronic gets near Zia, anything can happen!"

Zia walked calmly, but rather crossly, over to them.

"Thanks, Max," she said.

"Wait, where's my—" Max was about to ask what had happened to his fly, but his attention was drawn to the strange sounds coming from Zia's jacket – Kismet was gnawing on the robotic fly, which was still buzzing away pathetically.

"Hey!" he complained prising the chewed robot away from the cat.

"She can't help it," said Zia, thinking of Jack's

earlier defence of Buster. "It's what cats do."

Max was about to object when his R-phone buzzed, as did Zia's and Jack's.

"It's a Museum Club message," Jack announced. "Mr Cain needs us at the RBI base straight away. He says we might be terrified, but he's spelt it wrong." The RBI was secret within Ripley High; the agents were the only students who knew of its existence. In order to keep his messages calling the members to come together secret, Mr Cain would code them as 'Museum Club'. However, he was usually unable to resist sending them a clue as to what their latest mission would be.

▶▶ **SENDER:**
Mr Cain

▶▶ **SUBJECT:**
Museum Club

▶▶ **MESSAGE:**
Prepare to be pterofied!

The three agents quickly left the menagerie and headed back to the school.

"Wait!" said Zia, as they walked through the large front doors of the Ripley High building that had, at one time, been a private house. "I have to go and drop ... something off at my room." She was going to say Kismet, as the winged cat was still hidden inside her jacket, but she was worried that she might be overheard.

"You'd better be quick then," said Jack. "We'll cover for you with Mr C."

Zia nodded her thanks to the boys, when a loud voice stopped all three of them.

"You three! Stop right there. This time, I know you're up to no good," boomed Mr Clarkson.

2

Crazy Creature

"What could you possibly mean, Sir?" asked Max, putting on his most innocent-looking face, which for Max was not very innocent at all.

"I can smell something," said Mr Clarkson, his nose twitching like one of Buster's. "Something that smells like bad show." He moved closer to the agents, sniffing. "And that bad show smells like ... cat!"

The caretaker shouted the last word as the boys moved together, blocking Zia. She didn't need Kobe's telepathic tendencies to know what they were doing. Quickly, she bent down and unzipped her jacket, letting Kismet out and gently touching the cat to let her know she should run off and play, which is exactly what she did.

"What are you doing?" Mr Clarkson asked, seeing Zia bending down.

"Just tying my shoelace, Sir," said Zia. She stood back up to see Kismet run down the hall behind Mr Clarkson, her wings flapping. After a moment, she rose off the floor into the air.

"Cat?" asked Max. "There's no such thing!"

Jack and Zia winced at Max's silly response. Max was very used to trying to talk himself out of trouble, although he tended to talk himself into more trouble than he got out of. He seemed to realise he had said the wrong thing, too.

"Er, I mean—"

"What he means," Jack took over, "is that we've just been to the menagerie, and there are lots of cats there."

"Yes," said Max, recovering and seeing an opportunity. "Mr Clarkson, I'm very impressed. You must really have such an amazing sense of smell that you picked up on the cats in the menagerie. Can you smell the monkeys, too?"

"I didn't think you liked animals," Mr Clarkson said to Max, not quite ready to believe his story. "What monkeys were you with?"

"I love animals!" Max insisted, looking hurt. "And I love monkeys! Especially that ... that gorilla ... um, the one who speaks in sign language ... I love ... um ..."

▶▶ Koko the gorilla has worked with researchers at the Gorilla Foundation in California for over 30 years. She now knows over 1,000 different expressions in sign language. In fact many great apes have been taught sign language, and they have even been known to teach each other.

"Koko," Jack added, helpfully.

"Yes, Koko," said Max. "I love Koko."

"Hmmm," said Mr Clarkson, suspiciously. "What was that?" A shout came from down the hall. Zia caught Jack's eye as they saw what had happened. Kismet, in her flight along a corridor, had come across some other Ripley High students, who weren't expecting to see a winged cat in mid-air.

"Uh, we have to go, Sir," said Jack, pulling the other two with him.

Mr Clarkson, however, didn't really notice. Instantly, he had turned off and was following the sound of whatever 'bad show' was disrupting his quiet corridor.

"What about Kismet?" said Zia in a worried whisper. "We can't just leave her. What if Mr Clarkson finds her?"

"I'd worry more about Mr Clarkson finding out you brought her here," said Max as they rushed off.

"Did you mean to spell terrified wrong?"

When Jack, Max and Zia arrived at the RBI base, Li was quizzing Mr Cain on the riddle he had sent with their Museum Club message.

"I didn't," said Mr Cain with a mysterious smile.

"He spelled it as in pterosaur," explained Kate. "Pterofied?"

"That's a very bad joke, Sir," said Alek. "And what has a flying reptile got to do with our next mission?"

"I thought it was quite clever," their teacher replied, smiling. "RIPLEY?" he called.

The holographic head of Robert Ripley appeared above the desk and greeted them all.

"I told him it was a bad joke too," said RIPLEY.

"I really thought that perhaps my English wasn't as good as I imagined," said Alek.

"So what is our mission?" asked Kobe.

"Something strange has been seen in the skies over London," said RIPLEY. "It could be a giant bird, a really large bat or some sort of flying reptile." He looked at Jack as he said the last bit, knowing Jack was the animal expert.

The large screen behind RIPLEY flashed

into life and a video started to play. A very shaky image of the sky came into view. Then a building, then a statue, then back to the sky.

"Why do people always film things on their phones?" asked Max, annoyed at the jumpy footage.

"Because people don't tend to carry professional video equipment around with them," Jack mocked.

"Well, they should," said Max.

"Ssh, what's that sound?" asked Li, focusing on the high-pitched noise that was coming from the screen.

"It's probably the phone," said Max.

Mr Cain shot Max a stern look, which silenced him immediately. "Li? What is it that you can hear?" he asked. Li was the RBI's music and sound expert and if she had heard something it might be important.

"Whoa!" shouted Max, breaking Li's concentration as he watched something moving on the screen.

"Crikey, what was that thing?" asked Jack.

A blurry image had shot across the scene. It was moving very fast, and it was in the air. Mr Cain rewound the footage a fraction and paused it as the flying thing appeared

▶▶ Pterosaurs were giant flying reptiles that lived on Earth over 60 million years ago. The biggest of them, Quetzalcoatlus, flew over North America 80 million years ago, and was far larger than any bird. It had a wingspan of up to 15 metres (almost twice the width of a tennis court) and a long pointed beak to eat meat and fish.

on the screen. The agents all crowded round the frozen image, trying to get a better look at what it was.

"I don't think that's any sort of bird," said Jack. "It's just too big."

"But it has wings," said Zia, pointing out the shape of the creature's wings.

"Perhaps it is a pterosaur, like Mr Cain thought."

"Are those some sort of feathers?" asked Kobe, indicating an orangey section of what looked like a wing.

"It looks like fire to me," said Alek.

"It certainly could be some sort of energy source," Max added. "This really blurry bit," Max felt he had to explain as the whole image was pretty blurry, "could be a heat haze."

"Maybe it's a robot?" said Zia.

Mr Cain nodded his approval at the agents' observations. He pressed 'play' and the creature again whizzed across the sky, the strange noise growing louder and then fainter as the fuzzy image moved in and out of view.

"Now Li, what do you think about that noise?" he asked.

"At first I thought it might be some sort of car engine," she said, "but it sounds smaller and more metallic, almost like a whirring. It actually sounds a bit like a vacuum cleaner!"

"It really could be that the sound has distorted through the recording," Max offered, building on his earlier point.

"You're right, it could," said Mr Cain. "That's why Li," he turned towards her, "you are going on this mission to see if you can find out any more by hearing the noise in person. Because we still don't know if this thing is robotic or biological, your ability to identify sounds will be really useful."

"And if it turns out to be a giant bat, Li can talk to it in sonar!" Max added helpfully.

"You're going too, Max," said Mr Cain. "If this is some sort of robot, you're the best person to look into that."

"But what if it is some sort of giant, prehistoric creature – like a pterosaur?" asked Jack.

"Then hopefully you'll be there to find out," said Mr Cain. "You, Jack, are going to be the third agent on the team."

"The person who shot this video was on their way to work," continued Mr Cain.

"And still half-asleep, by the looks of it," grumbled Max, objecting again to the quality of the footage.

"And it just so happens that they work in the Ripley's museum in London," said Mr Cain, ignoring him. "The team will be based there while they are investigating."

3

Supersonic Sensors

Jack, Max and Li, the three agents selected for the mission, went next door to Dr Maxwell's lab. Dr Maxwell was the only other teacher who knew about the RBI. As their resident gadget man and 'mad professor' (according to most of the agents), alongside his regular science classroom Dr Maxwell had a second lab in the futuristic basement of the building that was home to the RBI base.

"Oh Max, I'm glad you're here," said Dr Maxwell. "I've been having real trouble with level six of one of those games you lent me: Warriors of Fire."

"Let me guess," said Max. "You can't get into the fortress because the vicious guard dog keeps ripping your avatar to pieces?"

"Yes!" Dr Maxwell exclaimed. "How did you know? You've not been using one of those spying devices on me again, have you?"

"I had trouble at that part too, for a couple of minutes," said Max, coolly. "You have to try to tickle the dog's tummy."

"Well, I never would have thought of that!" said the professor, laughing. "That's the sort of advice I would have expected to get from Jack here."

"Yawn," said Li. As the RBI's computer expert, Max spent a lot of time in Dr Maxwell's lab, and the two had become quite good friends, especially since Max had discovered that his professor loved computer games almost as much as he did.

"Ah, yes, sorry," said Dr Maxwell. "Back to work."

He pulled out some strange devices that looked like thick felt-tip pens. There were three of them.

"Pens?" asked Li.

"No, they may look like pens, but they are my supersonic sensors," he explained. "They will use sound waves in the air to tell you when the creature you are tracking comes within range."

▶▶ In 2005, a 28-year-old man collapsed and died after playing the online multiplayer game Starcraft for 50 hours continuously at an internet café in Taegu, South Korea. He only took short toilet breaks, and it is thought that he died from heart failure due to exhaustion.

"What's their range?" asked Li.

"Whatever you set it to be," said Dr Maxwell. "You set the three sensors up in different parts of London and switch them on. They create laser-like lines linking with the others, which make a triangle. Anything within that triangle is in range."

"Ah, I see," said Li.

Dr Maxwell handed her a device that looked a bit like her R-phone but with a larger screen.

"The map will appear on here," he told her.

"Won't it just track everything and everyone in London that's inside the triangle?" asked

Jack. "How will it know to look for our flying thing?"

"Well, you'll have to make sure you get the sensors as high as possible," the professor told them. "That way it will only track things in the sky. Try to find the tallest buildings you can, and place the sensors there. Then they won't be high enough to track aircraft, but the creature we are looking for should be the only thing in the air at that height and size."

The agents nodded and Max put the tracking device into his bag.

"Shall we go to see Miss Burrows now?" asked Li. Miss Burrows was the team's geography and history teacher and although she didn't know that the RBI existed, the agents found that it was always worth speaking to her before a mission. Without knowing it, Miss Burrows helped them research the area they would be visiting.

"You two go ahead," said Max. "I'm going to

stay here and try to fix my fly."

"Your what?" asked Li, as Max pulled the chewed mechanical insect out of his pocket.

"Zia's cat tried to eat it," Max said sadly, as he put the still buzzing fly on the table.

"Oh well, it's not the end of the world," said Dr Maxwell encouragingly. "I'm sure you'll be able to mend it."

Max started to collect the things he would need, as Jack and Li left the lab.

"Hold it right there," Mr Cain called after the two agents as they headed toward the staircase out of the secret RBI base. They turned to face their teacher.

"We're about to go and see Miss Burrows," Li told him.

"Well, you might be, but Jack's not."

"Why not?" asked Jack, looking alarmed.

"Because you have to help Zia."

"Help Zia with what?" asked Jack.

"Mr Clarkson has had to go and deal with a group of screaming second-year girls," Mr Cain explained. "Apparently, they were being terrorised by a flying cat."

Jack felt his face flush with guilt.

"I'm sure it's nothing to do with you or Zia," said Mr Cain, although from his tone and the look on his face Jack could see that his teacher

knew it had everything to do with him and Zia. "However, you are our resident animal expert, and I know Zia is particularly fond of Kismet the winged cat, so I thought the pair of you would be only too glad to help."

"Of course, Mr C," Jack nodded.

"But that's not fair," said Li, trying to stand up for her friend. "Jack needs to come and see Miss—"

Jack threw her a sideways look knowing that Kismet's escape was partly his fault anyway. "It's fine, Li," he said. "You go and see Miss Burrows and I'll find out what she told you later."

"Good," said Mr Cain. "If that's settled, Jack, you can find Zia and the cat in the cafeteria."

Jack winced as he imagined the chaos that Kismet could have caused flying around."

4

Believe It or Not!

"Look, a London bus!" said Max, pointing as a large red double-decker, the sort that the city is famous for, drove past. It was closely followed by a black taxi, which was beeping its horn at the bus.

"It's so exciting here," said Jack. 'It's really loud and busy."

"It reminds me a bit of home," said Li, looking at the enormous buildings that rose up on either side of the road, making the street seem narrower. She had grown up in Beijing and was much more used to the hustle and bustle of city life than Jack.

"But how did we manage to hear the noise that the creature made so loudly on the video?" Jack asked, thinking to himself that London had been much quieter on the video.

"Mornings are often quieter, before all the tourists arrive," Li told him.

"Wow, look at that building," said Max, pointing to a large structure with ornate detailing around the windows and columns guarding the entrance. The huge building covered a whole block. As the agents turned a corner, they were met with a giant Ripley's Believe It or Not! sign.

"It looks like that's where the museum is, then," said Jack.

They walked closer to the entrance. Loud music was blaring from speakers and a huge inflatable of the tallest man in the world leaned out of one of the doors.

"It's like a party in there," said Li, looking at the invitingly bright lights.

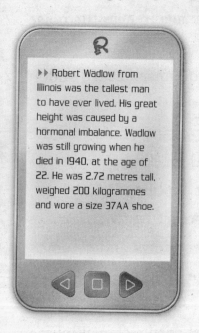

▶▶ Robert Wadlow from Illinois was the tallest man to have ever lived. His great height was caused by a hormonal imbalance. Wadlow was still growing when he died in 1940, at the age of 22. He was 2.72 metres tall, weighed 200 kilogrammes and wore a size 37AA shoe.

"Then why don't you come and join in?" asked a girl in a red 'Ripley's' polo shirt, as she stepped outside and greeted the agents.

"I think we just might," said Max, breaking into a huge grin.

"We're here from the RBI," Jack told her.

"Oh, my goodness!" she said, her enthusiasm obvious. "You're from the RBI? I'm so excited! Of course, we were told you would be coming, and I've been expecting you, but I can't believe you're actually here! I'm Abby." She held her hand out to introduce herself.

"I'm Jack," he shook her hand, "and this is Li and—"

"I'm Max," Max interrupted, leaping in front of Jack to shake Abby's hand.

"Are you here about the flying thing?" Abby asked.

"Yes, that's right," Li nodded.

"I saw it," said Abby. "It was really weird. And working here every day, I know weird!"

"Then it's you we need to speak to," Max told her.

"Well, and Sam. He sort of saw it too. Come in and we'll go and find him."

The agents followed Abby into the museum entrance and through a door marked 'staff only'. She bounced as she walked, her long dark hair swinging behind her. The agents followed her down a corridor, up a staircase and into a staff break room.

"Sam?" Abby called, as they entered the room. A young man with glasses looked up from his computer.

"The RBI is here to speak to us about that flying creature we saw!" Her smile had become even wider, if that was possible.

"Wow, the RBI?" said Sam. "I was just looking at websites to see if there were any reports

of anyone else seeing anything like we did. So far I can't find anything!"

Jack walked behind Sam and looked at the computer screen. Sam had been on a Ripley's website that had the local news and lots of unbelievable stories on it too. Jack pointed to an article about a winged cat.

"Wow, I wonder if that's an old story about

Kismet, or if it's another winged cat?" he said, making a note on his R-phone to investigate that story later. Another one caught his eye.

"Police baffled as unbelievable London robberies continue," he read. "Maybe we can solve those too if we've got time!" he said laughing.

Sam turned around to face Jack.

"So, you're really the RBI?" he asked. "I'd heard stories about you, but I didn't think you were real."

"We're real," said Jack. "'Believe it or not!'"

Max shook his head at Jack's joke and turned towards Abby. "So, tell us what happened."

"I was on my way to work," she began, "I had just come out of the tube station across the road from the museum. I was worried that I was going to be late. Then all of a sudden, there was this terrible noise."

"What did it sound like?" asked Li.

"It was horrible. It sounded like something out of some scary sci-fi horror movie. When I got to work Sam was on the ticket desk so I called for him to run down the road and see if he could still see it."

"I ran outside but there was nothing there really," said Sam. "Just a smoke trail in the air."

"I filmed the whole thing on my phone," added Abby. "Did you see the video I made? Was it useful?"

"It was really good," Max told her. "It gave us loads to go on."

Jack gave Max a quizzical look, remembering how much he had complained about the video when RIPLEY had shown it.

"Oh, I'm so pleased!" said Abby, beaming. "I was worried it might be a bit shaky. My phone is quite new."

"So, have you seen the creature again since?" asked Li. Abby shook her head.

"It must be somewhere around here," said

Jack. "It might even have some sort of lair nearby."

"Maybe it was just passing through," suggested Sam. "Perhaps it lives somewhere else?"

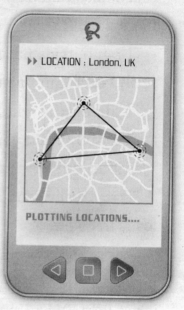

"It might do," agreed Li. "We should set up the tracking towers."

"We need to find the tallest buildings in London," said Max.

"Ooh, I'll go and get you a map," said Abby.

"I'll come with you," Sam offered. "My break's over." He turned to the RBI agents. "If you need anything else, you can find me in the shrunken head room."

"Thanks," said Jack.

"Most people are shocked when I tell them that I'm working with the shrunken heads," Sam laughed.

"Not us," said Li. "We have a shrunken head room at our school."

"Now that's amazing! I'd love to see them some time," Sam said smiling, as he and Abby left the room.

"They're really nice," said Li.

"Abby's pretty," said Max.

"Your video footage was really good, Abby," said Jack, mimicking Max.

"You're just jealous," Max teased. Jack started to protest, but then stopped as Abby came back into the room with a map.

"Let's split up," said Jack. "If we each take a sensor and place it on one of the tallest buildings, it will be faster. We'll decide where to go once we've seen a map. Then we'll meet back here afterwards."

The others nodded their agreement.

The three RBI agents met back at the Ripley's museum just as it began to get dark. Max was holding the receiver and the screen showed the triangle formed by the three towers.

"So this triangle covers most of London?" asked Li.

"A good portion of it," Max told her.

"And what's that dot?" asked Li, as a small blip appeared on the screen near one of their sensors.

"That might just be our flying creature," said Max.

5

Mini Madness

"If that's our creature, then it's moving very fast," said Jack, looking at the small dot as it made its way quickly across the illuminated screen.

"We'll need to hurry if we're going to catch it," said Li.

"How far is this on foot?" Max asked Abby. "Can we run it?"

Abby shook her head. "No, it's quite a way."

"Then how will we ever get there?" asked Li.

"Why don't you take the Mini?" suggested Abby. The agents looked at her, confused. "The crystal Mini," she added, pointing to one of the exhibits in the corner of the entrance hall: a Mini Cooper car covered in thousands of crystals. "Minis are great for getting around London. They're so small."

"Okay then, let's hurry," said Jack. "I'll drive."

"The only thing you'll have to worry about is the traffic lights," Abby warned. "There are quite a few around here."

▶▶ Artists Ken and Annie Burkitt used more than one million Swarovski crystals to cover a 2004 Mini Cooper car with pictures of American landmarks, including the Statue of Liberty and Mount Rushmore. It took six months to complete the work, placing each crystal on the car, one at a time.

"Leave that to me," said Max, climbing

into the passenger seat and pulling a small handheld computer out of his backpack. Soon, the agents were racing through the narrow streets of London in the Mini. Huge buildings loomed on either side of the road and the pavements were packed with people. Jack felt quite boxed in as he moved the car through the maze of roads.

"Traffic light!" he yelled, seeing a set of lights

ahead that were about to change.

"I'm on it," Max told him. Max's ability to do incredible things with computers meant that he had been able to hack into the London traffic system and control the lights. Every time the agents approached a set of red lights, Max would send a signal to change them to green. At the same time, he set the lights in all the other directions to red, stopping the rest of the

traffic until the agents, in their unbelievable car, were safely past.

"There are going to be some angry people," said Li, as she saw the traffic building up along the roads they passed.

"The creature is heading south!" shouted Max, holding the receiver for the triangulation tracking device and following the small blip that was moving across the screen. He was directing Jack towards it, but it kept moving. Every time the dot changed course, Max called out its new direction and Jack would try to catch up with it.

Jack now took the first turning he could to change their route again.

"It's moving towards the river now," called Max, as the blip moved across the screen until it was travelling along next to the River Thames.

"Hang on," said Jack, wrenching the Mini's steering wheel hard to the left. The car screeched as it turned sharply, almost missing the narrow side street that he was hoping to take.

"Turn right here," suggested Max. Jack did as he was asked, but immediately met cars heading towards them! Horns blared and lights flashed as Jack frantically tried to move the Mini out of the way of the oncoming cars. Li screamed as a large truck cut across their path.

Jack pulled up on to the pavement, blasting his own horn to warn the people walking there to move out of the way. He found himself heading straight towards a market area and couldn't stop the car before it drove right through a flower stand.

"Sorry!" Jack called out of the window, as the stall keeper shook his fist angrily at the Mini. He looked across to see Max clutching a bunch of flowers.

"They just landed in my lap!" he explained in answer to Jack's disapproving look. "I thought I might take them back for Abby."

"Just tell me which direction I should be driving!" Jack told him, annoyed that

Max didn't seem to be taking this very seriously.

"We need to turn right to get to the river. Drive through that outdoor cafe, that would be the quickest way."

Jack did as Max instructed and headed towards the cafe.

"Aim for that table," Max pointed to where a waiter was just delivering some food. "I could really do with a burger!"

Jack pulled the car away from the cafe at the last moment and skidded around it. One waiter dropped the tray he was carrying, more in shock at seeing the crystal-covered car than avoiding it, but other than that no one was disturbed.

"Spoilsport," grumbled Max. "Take that road there. Then you'll need to go left, then left, then right then, oh..." he paused.

"What?" Jack asked.

"It'll be fine," said Max. "So left, left, right, and then left."

Jack took the directions Max told him. "We still seem too high up for the river," he commented.

"Do we?" asked Max, but his voice sounded as if he already knew that.

Jack turned the final left and gasped at the sight ahead of him.

"Have we gone the wrong way?" he asked.

The car was heading towards a very steep set of stone steps.

"No, I think we're okay," Max said, still sounding very cool, as though he was expecting this.

"What about the steps?" Jack asked.

"We drive down them." Max broke into a huge grin as he made the suggestion. "It's the fastest way," he explained, seeing Jack's

excited look.

"Hang on then," said Jack. "Hold tight!"

In the back seat Li screwed her eyes tightly shut, held on to the seat and placed her feet firmly on the floor, bracing herself for the impact.

As the car juddered down the steps, the agents jostled up and down with it.

"I c-can fee-e-l e-v-ery bone in m-my bod-y-y bump-in-g," said Li, her voice shaking with the car.

The stairs turned a sharp corner and Jack turned the car with it, bumping the Mini down the second half of the stairs. People leapt out of the way with puzzled looks – a Mini driving down a flight of steps wasn't something you saw every day in London, and certainly not one covered from bumper to bumper in crystals!

At the bottom of the steps, the car drove back on to the road that was running next to the river.

"He's straight in front of us," said Max, noticing that the dot on the screen was very close. Jack speeded up and rocketed along beside the water. They rushed on forwards past many of London's bridges.

"We're closing in on it," said Max. "It should be right ahead of us!"

Jack looked up and saw the most famous of London's bridges, Tower Bridge.

"Wait a minute—" said Max. He was looking at the screen, but the dot seemed to have just disappeared. "Where's it gone?"

"Where's what gone?" asked Jack.

"Stop the car," Max told him. He jumped out of the passenger door and held the receiver up in the air, hoping that something had blocked the signal, and the dot would reappear.

"It's just gone," he said. "The dot, it's vanished."

Jack took the receiver and looked at it too. There was nothing there.

"The creature has obviously flown out of range," said Li.

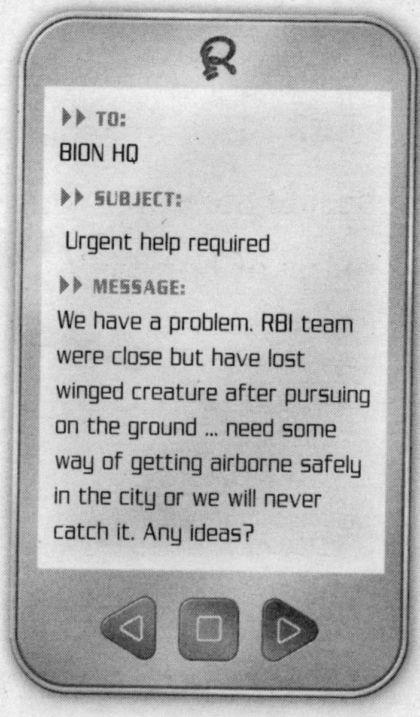

"It must have," agreed Max, still confused.

"I was driving my best," Jack told them, "but I just don't see how we can catch the creature if it's flying and we're trying to drive along busy London streets."

> ▶▶ TO:
> BION HQ
>
> ▶▶ SUBJECT:
> Urgent help required
>
> ▶▶ MESSAGE:
> We have a problem. RBI team were close but have lost winged creature after pursuing on the ground ... need some way of getting airborne safely in the city or we will never catch it. Any ideas?

"I think we should call BION Island for help," Jack suggested.

"Good idea," said Li. "Someone there will be able to think of something."

6

Squirrel Suits

The following morning, the agents arrived back at the Ripley's museum.

"RIPLEY said that he would be sending something to help us," Jack told the others.

"I wonder what he has thought up," said Li.

The agents were greeted by Abby, who was her normal cheery self.

"There's someone here to see you," she told them.

"Wow, RIPLEY must have worked out something really quickly," said Li, amazed.

Abby took the agents into the museum and to an area with lots of shelves that were stacked high with boxes, all labelled with what was inside them.

"These are all things that Mr Ripley found on his travels," Abby explained, as they made their way through the towering shelves.

"I don't think Rip found *him*," said Max, pointing at the figure leaning halfway inside one of the boxes, looking for something.

"It's Dr Maxwell," giggled Li, as their professor emerged from the box.

"I heard you could use some help," he said, "so I flew in overnight."

"Aren't you tired?" asked Li.

"No, if I don't get much sleep it's not the end of the world for me," he told them. "I'm used to staying up all night and working on inventions. Which reminds me ..." he started digging around in one of the boxes again. "I brought you these!" He pulled out what looked like ski suits.

"What are they?" asked Max.

"They're called 'squirrel suits', or 'wingsuits'," explained Dr Maxwell. "They are suits that can also act as parachutes. They have material sewn between the legs and under the arms." He stretched the suit out so the agents could see the extra material. "With these, you can jump off high buildings. The extra material will act as a parachute to slow your fall, but will also trap air and create lift, allowing you to travel further."

"They sound great," said Max. "But can we walk in them? Won't we trip over, as if our legs are tied together?"

"You shouldn't," said Dr Maxwell. "Why don't you try them on?"

The agents put on the suits. Li looked at herself in a big mirror, a broken pane from

▶▶ In April 2007, Jeb Corliss, American daredevil, flew in a wingsuit under the giant arm of the Jesus Christ statue that overlooks Rio de Janeiro, Brazil. He passed about a metre from the 36.5-metre structure at high speed after jumping out of a plane at a height of 4,500 metres.

the mirror maze that was being stored there.

"I look like a huge marshmallow," she complained as the trick glass distorted her shape. She turned to Dr Maxwell. "One day, I hope you're going to come to me with an amazing invention that is also fashionable and won't make me look really silly."

"Fashion's not really my thing, I'm afraid, Li," said Dr Maxwell.

"We inventors have much more important things to worry about than what the latest trend is," added Max.

Li looked at Dr Maxwell with his huge bushy hair and Max who always wore the same overalls, thinking to herself that it was quite obvious that neither of them worried too much about how they looked.

While the others were discussing fashion, or lack of fashion, Jack was taking some time to look at the labels of the things on the shelves.

"Tribal warrior mask, bubblegum bird,

fossilised dinosaur egg, tooth tattoos," he read out the tags that were tied to the objects or brown boxes that lined the shelves all around him.

In between two large brown boxes, Jack saw a flash of colour: something red and yellow peeped out at him. He decided that it was his duty as an RBI agent to investigate. Standing on tiptoe, he reached in behind the boxes. His hand grabbed something metallic and he pulled it out towards him. It was an intricately designed tin, very similar to four other tins that were stored in the secret RBI base back at Ripley High. Those tins had all been found by agents while on missions. In the Florida Everglades, Kobe had discovered an artefact that had once belonged to Robert Ripley and had gone missing from Ripley High. When they brought it back to BION Island, the artefact had launched them on an amazing quest. Rip had hidden special artefacts all around the

world and left clues to help those who followed him find the treasures. So far, every clue the agents had found had been in a red and yellow tin, just like the one Jack was now holding in his hand. He walked back to Dr Maxwell and the other agents with his discovery.

"It's a clue tin," said Li, recognising it at once. "Have you opened it?"

Jack shook his head. There was a label on the tin, similar to the ones on the other boxes, but instead of having a description of what was inside, it had a message on it: 'To those who follow me'.

"That looks like Rip's writing," said Li.

Jack looked around for Abby. The museum staff member was filing more exhibits two rows along.

"Where did this come from?" he asked her.

"I don't know," she admitted. "When the museum opened we received artefacts from lots of the other museums, and this must have come in with them.

"Can we open it?" asked Max.

"Of course," said Abby. "You're RBI agents – nothing here is off limits to you!"

Jack gently worked the lid off the tin and tipped its contents out into Li's hands.

"It's a book," she said, slightly puzzled. The book was a biography of a 1920s explorer.

"Eugh, it's a history book," complained Max. "How can this be a useful clue? Are there any pictures, at least?"

"I think it's important," said Li. "It's in a clue tin, and the message says that it's for those who follow Rip. That's the RBI – that's us! I'm going to contact Kate. She'll love it, and I bet she'll find something in there that will finally lead us to that hidden artefact."

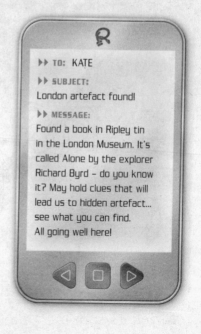

▶▶ TO: KATE

▶▶ SUBJECT:
London artefact found!

▶▶ MESSAGE:
Found a book in Ripley tin in the London Museum. It's called Alone by the explorer Richard Byrd – do you know it? May hold clues that will lead us to hidden artefact... see what you can find. All going well here!

"Before you do that, I still have something else to show you," said Dr Maxwell.

He was holding a hook attached to a long rope.

"It's a grappling hook," said Jack. "I've used those before on trips into the outback with my dad."

"Ah, but this isn't just any grappling hook," said Dr Maxwell. "It's a magnetic grappling hook."

"Like in Treasures of the Amazon?" asked Max, referring to one of his computer games.

"Exactly like that," said Dr Maxwell.

"Well then, I've used one of those heaps of times." Max turned to the others. "It works in pretty much the same way as regular grappling hooks. You throw the hook and it latches on to something. But the magnet means that it will attach itself to metal much more easily. And see this button?" he pointed to a small button at the end of the rope. "If you press this, the magnet and the hook let go. It's really useful if you've used the hook to swing across a fiery canyon on to a bridge and need to get your hook back."

"I doubt there'll be much swinging across canyons on to bridges," said Li. She couldn't believe the way Max thought that if he'd done something in a computer game it meant that he'd really done it.

"But it will be useful for helping you get to

the top of high things so that you can jump off them in your wingsuits," said Dr Maxwell. "I suggest that you wait until tonight and then find some good, high spots to start on."

"Why should we wait till tonight?" asked Max.

"Every sighting RIPLEY had catalogued for this creature is at night, or early in the morning," said Dr Maxwell. "Also it will be much easier for you to fly around at night without everyone in London noticing you and wondering what's going on! Teenagers in flying suits aren't an everyday sight, you know!"

"We know that something strange happened near Tower Bridge," Max reminded the others. "I think we should each take up a position near there. I'm sure it has something to do with the flying creature."

The other agents agreed.

7

Fantastic Flights

As night fell, the agents were all in position. Li was waiting on the huge clock that rang the hour for the British Houses of Parliament. Big Ben had already chimed once and Li, with her supersensitive hearing, wished that she had chosen a quieter location.

When she heard a strange whirring sound, at first she wondered if it was the ringing in her ears that had been caused by the bell, but then she realised that she had heard this sound before, in a video. It was the noise that Abby's camera phone had recorded when the flying creature had appeared!

As the sound grew louder Li leaped from the clock tower, hoping to catch up with whatever was making the strange noise. Her suit caught the air and she soared like a bird into the night sky, surrounded by the lights from the city's amazing buildings.

Li was just getting used to the feeling when the creature appeared to her left. It was huge! It didn't look like any sort of bird, or animal she had ever seen. Using the radio in her RBI wingsuit, she radioed to the other two agents that she had seen the creature and was chasing it.

"Jack, you really have to see this!" she exclaimed. "It's like nothing I've ever seen before. I just hope that you know what sort of animal it is."

"Should I move towards you?" Jack asked. He was waiting on the London Eye, the massive wheel on the banks of the River Thames that gave passengers a bird's eye view of London.

"No, I'll try to bring it to you," Li told him. As soon as she said it though, the creature turned away and headed back towards the city. Li chased after it, but it speeded up, as if it knew it was being followed and was trying to lose its shadow.

As Li followed the creature through the urban jungle of London town, she realised that she was beginning to lose height. The wingsuit had allowed her to travel quite a distance, but gravity was pulling her back down to earth. As best she could, Li herded the creature back through the maze of skyscrapers and monuments to the river. They were just about to pass the London Eye as she landed on the ground beside the water.

"It's all yours, Jack," she said over the microphone.

"I've got it," said Jack as he swooped off the big wheel and into the air. "We're heading towards you, Max."

The creature flew straight along the river now, rising to fly over the bridges. Jack did his best to keep up, remembering everything he knew about the way birds and bats moved to help him maintain height. He was also racking his brain to think of anything he knew about flying creatures to help explain what this thing could be. A couple of times, Jack thought he saw what looked like fire surrounding the creature's wings, lighting up the dark sky around it. He thought about fiery mythical creatures, like the phoenix and dragons that breathed fire, and wondered if whatever this was could be the basis for some of those stories. Jack had heard about animals that had lived for millions of years undiscovered in some of the world's rainforests; perhaps this was one of those. However, it still didn't explain what it was doing in a big city.

The creature began to duck under bridges as well as flying over them, and Jack followed it. It wasn't until after he had flown under the second bridge that he realised what was happening. The flying thing knew it was being followed and knew how his suit worked. Having lowered himself almost to water level to go under the last bridge, Jack wasn't able to raise himself again to fly over the next one.

"He's all yours, Max," said Jack, seeing Tower

Bridge not too far in front of him.

"Got it," said Max.

Jack used the little height he had left to direct himself to the edge of the water. He touched down in the middle of the terrace of an expensive-looking restaurant and diners looked up from their plates in amazement as he swooped in. Jack waved to let them know

everything was all right and left as soon as he could.

As soon as he heard Jack's message, Max leaped off from his position on Tower Bridge. He saw the creature a little way down the river, quite low to the water, and thought about how he would get to it before it passed under the bridge. He knew the extra material in his suit worked like a parachute and slowed the speed at which he would fly. So, if he pulled his arms in and kept his legs together, he would simply fall. Max did just that; he fell towards the ground like a missile, only opening up the suit when the water seemed dangerously close.

As he did so, Max heard a loud ripping sound. He looked to the side and saw that the material in his suit had torn. The speed at which he had been falling had been so great that when he opened the wings the pressure

of the air had ripped through them. There was now nothing to slow his fall and he was heading fast, much too fast, towards the black dark water that lay only a short distance below him.

8

Robofly Returns

Max's arms and legs thrashed wildly as he panicked, seeing the hard sheet of water coming ever closer. He screwed his eyes shut, ready for the impact of his body hitting the river, which at this speed would have the same effect as hitting a brick wall; but instead, he felt himself being lifted gently back into the air.

Max looked up and saw a black shape looming above him in the darkness. He went back to waving his arms around and screaming. He did not want to be taken back to this huge, hideous bird's lair for supper! Fire erupted around him, Max tried to make his shouts even louder, calling for help from anyone who could possibly hear him.

On the river in front of them, Max saw a boat taking the city's rubbish to a dump. He thought that if only he could free himself he could land on the boat and let it carry him to safety. He shook and squirmed as much as he possibly could, still screaming for someone to rescue him. The boat got nearer and Max felt himself being lowered towards it. He wriggled even more and felt the thing's grip on him loosen.

As he finally freed himself and struggled on to the boat, Max thought that he heard a voice. He looked around and saw the creature flying away.

Max shivered at the thought of what the creature might have done to him had he let it carry him off.

"Max, up here!" he heard Li's voice from a bridge a little way down the river and looked through the darkness to see the other two RBI agents waving RBI-issue strobe lights and calling to him. Not wanting the others to think that he had been scared, Max smiled in case they could see him through the darkness, pretending that everything was fine and unhooked his grappling hook from where it had been stowed in his suit.

He skilfully swung the hook up towards the bridge, pressing the button that would magnetise the hook. It stuck fast to the iron

bridge and Max was able to swing himself up and over the side.

Once he had climbed to safety he pressed the button again, releasing the hook and reeling the whole thing in.

▶▶ The extreme sport of bridge swinging involves willing participants hurling themselves off high bridges and swinging like a pendulum on a rope under the bridge at speeds approaching 80 kilometres an hour, often dangerously close to the ground.

"I told you we'd need to swing on to bridges," he told Li.

"We were so worried," she told him, ignoring his comment. "We saw that creature grab you and thought it was going to carry you away."

"It would have, if I hadn't kept so cool and made it release me," Max shrugged.

"Yeah, you were cool, alright," Jack smirked. He waved his arms about and jumped from leg to leg. "Someone save me!" he yelled in an imitation of Max. "What were you doing, diving off that bridge without using your suit properly?" he asked. Jack had been worried about his best friend and now Max was safe, Jack was cross at how silly he had been.

"I thought it would be faster," said Max.

Jack tried to calm himself, realising that there was no point getting annoyed with Max; they all knew how stubborn and reckless he could be.

"It looked more like the creature rescued you," Jack laughed. "If you'd hit that water at that speed, you'd have been a goner."

Max gulped. He knew Jack was right, but he didn't really want to admit his mistake.

The agents ran to their car and made their way back to the Ripley's museum where Abby ran up to them with news.

"There's been another robbery," she told them. "The newspapers are reporting that the flying creature is behind them."

"It couldn't have been," said Jack. "The creature was busy rescuing Max."

"It didn't rescue me," said Max, sensing everyone's eyes on him and feeling a bit silly. "It tried to take me to its lair."

"It's a shame it couldn't rescue us from that smell," said Li. "Phew!"

"It's not my fault!" said Max. "It was the garbage boat I landed on!"

"Did you find the creature's lair?" asked Dr Maxwell, changing the subject.

"No," Jack replied. "It got away."

"I still think it's some sort of prehistoric creature, maybe a pterosaur," said Jack. "But how on earth could such a creature commit robberies? That's ridiculous! None of this makes any sense."

"Well that's what they're saying," said Abby.

"We need to find that creature even more now," said Li.

"But how can we? We have no idea where it went," said Jack. He looked at the map linked to the supersonic sensors. "The creature doesn't even seem to be in the area we can track now."

"We can still track it," said Max. He pulled his R-phone out of his pocket. After pressing a few buttons a map came up, similar to the one they had used to track the creature earlier.

"What's that?" asked Li.

"When the creature grabbed me, I put a tracker on him," Max explained. "Something small that will stay with him and allow us to follow him."

"Don't tell me you stuck robofly on him?" laughed Jack.

"Yes, I did," said Max. The fly that Jack had tormented Zia with back at Ripley High was now tracking the creature and reporting its location back to Max.

"You're a genius," Jack smiled.

9

Towers and Terrors

"Robofly is beeping!" shouted Li, pointing at Max's R-phone, which was vibrating and making loud noises to alert them.

"It's at Tower Bridge again," said Max.

The three RBI agents rushed to the bridge, once again driving the crystal-covered Mini at speed through the streets of London.

When they arrived at Tower Bridge, the agents pulled out their magnetic grappling hooks and started to climb up the side of one of the towers. Robofly's signal was telling them that they were getting close. Max swung himself towards one of the tower windows, which was ajar, but his magnetic hook

just missed.

"Max," shouted Li in alarm as she saw her friend falling. She reached out for him, but he had already passed her.

As he began to fall he threw his hook upwards again, and felt it snag on something.

A yell from above him told him that it was Jack!

"Careful," said Jack once Max appeared beside him, having reeled himself up again. "That was very nearly my foot you hooked on to."

More carefully this time, Max swung his hook through the tower window and followed it inside

"Wow, check this out!" he called back to the others.

Jack and Li appeared through the open window and took in the scene that had amazed Max. It was a small room and every wall was covered in posters. Some were from films, some were comic book pictures and others looked as if they were drawn by hand. All the posters were of superheroes. The floor was littered with comics, all with pictures of heroes on the cover, flying through the air or ready to fight the villain.

"This is amazing," said Max. "Some of these comics are really rare and hard to get hold of."

In the corner of the room stood two dummies, like those that display clothes in menswear shops. One of them was wearing a suit. It looked like somebody's homemade version of a comic book superhero suit: it had a headpiece and mask, with large goggles attached to it. Max felt sure he had seen the mask somewhere before. Strapped on to the

▶▶ One of the most expensive comics in the world, Action Comics No. 1, introduced Superman for the first time in 1938. A copy was sold for $195,000 in 2004.

▶▶ In 2009, a collection of 3,000 comic books worth over $1 million was discovered in a house that sold for just $65,000 in St Louis, Missouri, USA!

suit was a huge pair of collapsible fibreglass wings. They spanned almost half the length of the room and had something else attached to them. As the agents moved closer, they saw that each wing had a mini gas turbine stuck to the fibreglass.

"I thought I saw fire," said Jack. "Would you

believe it! Our creature is a person who appears to be wearing an extraordinary flying suit."

"It's a pretty amazing flying suit," added Max. "I wish I'd invented one like this. Those wings are huge, yet it looks like they can collapse to be really small. That must be how he gets them in and out of the room."

"I wonder why the second dummy isn't wearing a suit?" asked Jack.

Before anyone could answer Li held up a hand to silence them, she had heard something.

"Wait, what's that?" asked Li, turning her head to the side so that her incredible hearing could pick out the noise she was listening for. "It sounds like someone running up stone steps." She pointed in the direction the sound was coming from and the agents saw a small door. They all went through it to find a staircase rising up to the top of the tower. The agents quickly ran up it, when an alarm sounded.

"Where is that coming from?" asked Li,

clasping her hands over her ears.

"I'd say over there," said Max, as he exited the stairway on to the roof. He pointed to the roof of the building opposite: the Tower of London. As they looked, the other agents saw people on the roof of the tower, wearing ski masks to hide their faces. Lights were flashing and sirens were wailing all around them.

"They must be the thieves," said Li.

The thieves were waving and pointing at something in the sky. It was the person in the flying suit – probably the one who had been running up the stairs ahead of them.

"Stop, thieves!" he shouted, loud enough for the agents on the nearby bridge tower to hear.

The thieves looked petrified of the huge winged creature that had appeared in the sky above them.

They panicked and tried to run away, but in

their confusion kept crashing into each other.
They were already on the roof and had nowhere

else to go.

"You are surrounded. Throw down your
weapons and surrender," boomed the birdman.

The thieves immediately did as they were told
dropping their weapons and bags to the floor.

Stolen jewels spilled out all over the roof and glinted in the light that the birdman's flaming burners were shining down on to the scene.

The RBI agents watched from the top of Tower Bridge as the man in the wingsuit slowly moved closer and closer to the cowering thieves.

Sirens approached growing louder and louder.

'The police are here," said Li.

Moments later police ran onto the roof and handcuffed the thieves.

"He really did it," said Max, impressed. "He really stopped the robbery."

10

Birdman

The RBI agents ran as quickly as they could down from the tower and over to the growing chaos around the Tower of London.

Some media vans with journalists and photographers had arrived and everyone was crowding around the police and the thieves. The RBI agents weren't interested in this. They looked around but couldn't see the man in the suit anywhere.

"This way," said Li hearing a noise that she instantly recognised as the suit's engines cooling down. The others followed Li as she ran into a dark alleyway, where they all came face to face with the man in the suit.

"You're amazing!" said Max, his voice full of admiration as they approached the man. "I wish I had a suit as good as yours. How did you make it? Is it difficult to fly? How does it work?"

The man answered all of Max's questions and then the agents interviewed him for the database to find out who he was and what he was doing. He told them his name was Marc Powell and he was a bridge operator at Tower Bridge. It was his job to raise the bridge to let ships pass through. He had always been a huge fan of superheroes and comic books, and the tower operator's room seemed like the perfect base for a superhero. Marc was also really good with electronics. As a trained engineer, part of his role was to make sure all the historical

mechanisms on the bridge kept working. In his spare time, he had decided to make his dream come true and create a superhero outfit for himself. All good superheroes needed to fly and so he had found a way to give himself jet-powered wings that would lift him into the air.

After hearing about the robberies that were

happening throughout London, he had decided that he could really be of help and that this was the ideal time to launch his superhero, 'Birdman'. However, it all went wrong when people started to think that he was behind the robberies. He was desperate to find the real villains and to clear his name.

▶▶ Superbarrio is a real life South American superhero. The mystery figure, who dresses in a tight red costume, cape and wrestling mask, has stood up for the rights of the poor and the homeless in Mexico for over a decade. He does not use violence, but organises protests and petitions instead.

"But you could have been killed," said Li, amazed at the man's bravery.

"I just wanted to help people," he told them. "I had made this amazing suit and it was just sitting there."

Jack explained about the RBI and the Ripley's database. "You can certainly help us! You and your suit are certainly worthy of an entry in the database," he said. "That suit is absolutely amazing!"

"I wonder if we could make some suits like this for ourselves?" Max asked. "Would we be able to get the design?"

"Of course," said Marc. "If I can help more people that would be wonderful."

They walked back towards Tower Bridge as they talked. Pausing for a moment outside the Tower of London, they saw the thieves being put into police cars, their hands cuffed together.

Li looked at her watch.

"We had better hurry," she told the others. It's going to be pretty busy getting through all the traffic around the Tower of London now."

"We really need to look at inventing something that could just transport us somewhere," said Max.

"Funny you should mention that," said Marc. "I've been thinking of a similar idea for a while and my next invention should be finished in a few months."

"Oh no," groaned Li. "Just make sure you contact us about it first next time!"

RIPLEY'S DATABASE ENTRY

RIPLEY FILE NUMBER : 54763

MISSION BRIEF : Believe it or not, a strange creature has been seen in the skies above London. Investigate accuracy of these accounts for Ripley database.

CODE NAME : The Birdman

REAL NAME : Marc Powell

LOCATION : London, England

AGE : 39

HEIGHT : 178 cm

WEIGHT : 70 kg

VIDEO CAPTURE

UNUSUAL CHARACTERISTICS :

Wears a suit that has huge, collapsible, fibreglass wings with mini gas-turbine engines strapped to them. When in flight, flames can be seen coming from the engines.

RBI DATABASE APPROVED!

INVESTIGATING AGENTS :

Max Johnson, Jack Stevens, Li Yong

▶▶ YOUR NEXT ASSIGNMENT

JOIN THE RBI IN THEIR NEXT ADVENTURE!

Sub-Zero Survival

Prologue

A cold wind blew fiercely across the frosty wilderness, where white mounds of snow covered everything in sight. Stars shone brightly in the black sky. With no human civilisation for miles, there was no man-made light to pollute the brilliance of this night scene. A chilling gale moving in from the water whipped up the surface of this truly hostile land. A group of seals sensed the change in the wind and barked to each other, giving and receiving orders. Although this place was far too harsh for man, the seals thrived in the bitter, glacial conditions. One by one, the creatures moved towards the edge of the ice floe they were on and dropped into the biting cold water below.

A dark shape cut silently through the water heading for the seals: a killer whale, hungry for a meal. It targeted a small cluster of seals on

the edge of the group as its best option and set off through the icy sea towards them.

At the last moment, the whale changed its course. Some other creature had blocked its path, a pale body rising between the whale and its prey. The seals, sensing danger, began to bark again and scurried away. The confused whale backed off for now, realising that this disruption had taken away the advantage of surprise and allowed its meal to escape.

As the whale disappeared back into the icy waters, the pale creature joined the group of seals again. The seals swam happily beside this newcomer, a creature quite uncommon in this land of ice, and almost unbelievable in the glacial water.

▶▶

ENTER THE STRANGE WORLD OF RIPLEY'S ...

▶▶ Believe it or not, there is a lot of truth in this remarkable tale. The Ripley's team travels the globe to track down true stories that will amaze you. Read on to find out about real Ripley's case files and discover incredible facts about some of the extraordinary people and places in our world.

Ripley's Believe It or Not!®

▶▶ JET MAN

credit: Anja Niedringhaus/AP/Press Association Images

An ex-airline pilot, Yves Rossy, doesn't need a plane to fly anymore. The daredevil from Switzerland can soar thousands of metres up in the air attached to his homemade wings powered by four miniature jet engines.

▶▶ The wings unfold automatically while he is airborne after jumping from a regular aircraft, before the jet turbines activate. He steers with his body weight and lands using a parachute.

▶▶ After leaping from a plane at 3,000 metres, Yves flew 35 kilometres across the English Channel in 2008, reaching speeds of over 300 kilometres an hour.

▶▶ Yves attempted to be the first person to fly between two continents – Africa and Europe, from Spain to Morocco – but hit turbulence and was forced to ditch into the sea in 2009.

LONDON SIGHTS

TOWER BRIDGE

▶▶ Tower Bridge was built in 1894 when the population of the east side of the city increased so that another bridge, apart from London Bridge, was needed for people to cross the River Thames. It took eight years and 432 workers to build. The lower road is made up of two halves that can be raised to allow tall ships through.

▶▶ Big Ben is a large clock that stands at the end of the Palace of Westminster. Built in 1859, the tower is over 96 metres high.

THE TOWER OF LONDON

▶▶ The Tower of London was built over 900 years ago by William the Conqueror. It stands 27.5 metres high and some walls are 3.3 metres thick. It was the tallest building in London for 212 years.

THE LONDON EYE

▶▶ The London Eye carries 800 passengers, and from the top of the ride on a clear day you can see as far as 40 kilometres away. Each of the capsules weighs 10 tons and each rotation takes about 30 minutes. The wheel moves continuously, allowing passengers to step on and off without stopping.

CASE FILE #002

▶▶ CRYSTAL MINI

Artists Ken and Annie Burkitt from Canada entirely covered a Mini Cooper car in over one million Swarovski crystals that depict 11 American icons, such as the Statue of Liberty, the White House and Mount Rushmore.

▶▶ It took a team of four people six months to attach the colourful crystals one by one.

▶▶ Despite the many sparkling additions, the car is still a fully functioning Mini Cooper.

▶▶ The artists have also covered a double-decker London bus in 100,000 gold-plated British pennies.

▶ FLIERS

PTEROSAURS

credit: Michael Burke/Rex Features

▶▶ Pterosaurs lived over 200 million years ago, and were some of the first animals to be able to fly. They included the largest creatures ever to get off the ground. *Hatzegopteryx* had an estimated wingspan of 12 metres and a head that measured 2.5 metres.

▶▶ The Arctic tern flies over 70,000 kilometres each year between the Arctic and the Antarctic, the longest migration of any bird. Over the possible 30-year lifetime of the bird, it can travel more than a million kilometres.

▶▶ The peregrine falcon is the fastest animal on earth. When seeking prey, it reaches speeds of more than 320 kilometres an hour during its 'power-dive' (called a stoop), as it swoops down to catch its prey in mid-air.

▶▶ The great albatross, which ranges across the Southern Oceans, has the largest wingspan of any living bird, measuring up to 3.3 metres. It spends most of its life in the air and can glide for hours without beating its wings.

▶▶ The bar-tailed godwit, a Pacific coastal bird, makes flights of more than 11,000 kilometres without stopping to eat.

▶▶ WINGSUIT MAN

credit: Sipa Press/Rex Features

▶▶ The suit works on the same principles that allow small mammals such as flying foxes to soar through the air from tree to tree.

Skydiver Ueli Gegenschatz used a hi-tech suit with extra fabric between the arms and legs, which acted like the wings of a bird. He travelled great distances with no propulsion other than the wind.

▶▶ Using only his wingsuit, Ueli flew an incredible 17.5 kilometres over the Irish Sea from the island Inis Mor to the Irish mainland.

▶▶ It took Ueli only 5 minutes 45 seconds to reach Ireland at an average speed of 250 kilometres an hour – fast enough to beat a passenger plane flying the same route.

▶▶ Ueli jumped from a plane at 4,500 metres to complete his flight.

►► RIPLEY

►► In his lifetime, Ripley travelled over 750,000 kilometres looking for oddities – the distance from Earth to the Moon and back again.

►► Ripley had a large collection of cars, but he couldn't drive. He also bought a Chinese sailing boat, called Mon Lei, but he couldn't swim.

►► Ripley was so popular that his weekly mailbag often exceeded 170,000 letters, all full of weird and wacky suggestions for his cartoon strip.

►► He kept a boa constrictor 8.5 metres long as a pet in his New York home.

►► Ripley's Believe It or Not! cartoon is the longest-running cartoon strip in the world, read in 42 countries and 17 languages every day.

In 1918, Robert Ripley became fascinated by strange facts while he was working as a cartoonist at the *New York Globe*. He was passionate about travel and, by 1940, had visited no less than 201 countries, gathering artefacts and searching for stories that would be right for his column, which he named Believe It or Not!

Ripley bought an island estate at Mamaroneck, New York, and filled the huge house there with unusual objects and odd creatures that he'd collected on his explorations,

RIPLEY'S
RBI
FACT OR FICTION?
BUREAU OF INVESTIGATION

▶▶

PACKED WITH FUN & GAMES,
THE **RBI** WEBSITE IS HERE!
CHECK IT OUT

REVIEWS

DOWNLOADS

MAPS & DATA

MORE TEAM TALK

FUN!

THE NEXT FILES

Check out the next amazing,
action-packed adventure
with the RBI team in ...

▶▶ Sub-Zero Survival

www.ripleysrbi.com

CLASSES IN MODERN SOCIETY

Classes in
Modern Society

T. B. BOTTOMORE

London
GEORGE ALLEN & UNWIN
Boston   Sydney

FIRST PUBLISHED IN 1965
NINTH IMPRESSION 1978

GEORGE ALLEN & UNWIN LTD
40 Museum Street, London WC1A 1LU

© *George Allen & Unwin (Publishers) Ltd., 1965*

ISBN 0 04 323001 6

PRINTED IN GREAT BRITAIN
in 10 point Baskerville type
BY UNWIN BROTHERS LIMITED
OLD WOKING, SURREY

PREFACE

This introduction to the study of social classes differs in several respects from the essay which I published under the same title in 1955, and which has been out of print for a number of years. I have used the opportunity of publishing an enlarged version of the work to discuss more fully the sociological theories of class, to include more material on class differences, and to take account of changes during the past decade in the social conditions and policies of the industrial countries. My re-examination of these problems has led me to conclusions which differ on some points from those which I expressed in 1955; and I have now attempted, in the concluding chapter, to set out more fully my view of the political and cultural significance of social classes in the modern industrial societies.

T. B. BOTTOMORE

March 1965

CONTENTS

I

Introduction

The division of society into classes or strata, which are ranged in a hierarchy of wealth, prestige and power is a prominent and almost universal feature of social structure which has always attracted the attention of social theorists and philosophers. During the greater part of human history this inequality among men has been generally accepted as an unalterable fact. Ancient and medieval writers, when they touch upon the subject of the social hierarchy, always tended to provide a rationalization and justification of the established order, very often in terms of a religious doctrine concerning the origin of social ranks. This is most apparent, perhaps, in the Hindu religious myths about the formation of the caste system. On the other side, the sporadic rebellions of the poor and oppressed were usually revolts against particularly irksome conditions rather than against the whole system of ranks, and they did not give rise to any clear conceptions of an alternative form of society.

Only in modern times, and particularly since the American and French Revolutions, has social class, as a stark embodiment of the principle of inequality, become an object of scientific study, and at the same time of widespread condemnation in terms of new social doctrines. The revolutionary ideal of equality, however variously it was interpreted by nineteenth-century thinkers, at least implied an opposition to hereditary privileges and to an immutable hierarchy of ranks. The revolutions of the late eighteenth century and the early nineteenth century, directed against the legal and political privileges which survived from the system of feudal estates, brought about an extension of civil and political rights and a greater degree of equality of opportunity. But at the same time they created a new social hierarchy, based directly upon the possession of

wealth, and this in turn came to be attacked during the nineteenth century by socialist thinkers who believed that the ideal
of equality ultimately implied a 'classless society'.

During the past 100 years great changes have taken place
in the social structure of the advanced industrial countries.
The history of this period can be seen in part as a record of
the growth of equality in new spheres of social life, or as some
writers have expressed it, of the growth of citizenship.[1]
Laissez-faire capitalism—and especially the doctrine of *laissez
faire* which was far more extreme than the practice—has more
or less vanished; and in all the industrial countries there is
some degree of central economic planning, some attempt to
regulate the distribution of wealth and income, and a more or
less elaborate public provision of a wide range of social services.
But there are important differences between the two principal
types of industrial societies, the Western capitalist societies[2]
and the Soviet-type societies of eastern Europe. In the former,
there has been a gradual and limited movement towards 'classlessness', which is usually held to be especially marked in the
past two decades—the era of the Welfare State—and which
has resulted from changes in the relative earnings of different
occupational groups and in rates of taxation, improvements in
education and social services, increasing opportunities for individual social mobility, and perhaps most of all, from the
recent rapid growth in total national income. These changes
will be examined more closely in a later chapter, but it is clear
at once that they do not amount to an abolition of social
classes. The Western societies are still capitalist, in the sense

[1] See especially T.H. Marshall, *Citizenship and Social Class* (1950).

[2] I use the terms 'capitalism' and 'capitalist society' as they are habitually
used by economic historians and sociologists, to refer to an economic and
social system existing during a particular historical period, which is
characterized principally by freedom of the market, free labour (i.e. individuals who are legally free and economically compelled to sell their labour
power on the market), and private ownership of the means of production
by industrial enterprises. These, together with secondary characteristics,
make it possible to distinguish with reasonable clarity between capitalism
and other types of society, such as feudalism, or socialist society. This is not
to say, however, that actual capitalist societies have remained unchanged
since their origins, that there are not sub-types of capitalism, or that mixed
and transitional forms of society cannot occur. Some of these problems will
be discussed more fully later in this book.

that their economic systems are dominated by privately owned industrial enterprises and that very pronounced social differences exist between the group of industrial property-owners and the group of wage-earners.

In the Soviet-type societies, on the other hand, the claim is made that social classes, or at least the hierarchical class structure, have disappeared with the abolition of private ownership of the means of production; and that the construction of a classless, socialist society is under way. This claim was not at first very closely examined, even by the critics of Soviet society, who concentrated their attention, during the Stalinist period, upon more blatant features of the social system—the repression of personal freedom and the prevalence of coercion and terror. Indeed, it seems to have been quite widely held at one time that the political dictatorship itself could be explained—in terms of an antithesis between liberty and equality—as a consequence of the attempt to enforce an unnatural equality of condition upon the members of society. But this was seen to be implausible when it was realized that there were great social inequalities in the Soviet-type societies; and in more recent studies the discussion has centred upon the emergence of a 'new ruling class' in these societies, and upon comparisons between the characteristics of élite groups in the Western and Soviet societies.

It is the main purpose of this book to consider how the movement towards social equality which began with the eighteenth-century revolutions has affected the social hierarchy in the industrial societies, and how, in turn, it has been influenced by the development of modern industry. This calls, in the first place, for an inquiry into the nature of modern social classes. It requires, secondly, a comparative study of the changes in social stratification which have occurred in the two principal types of industrial society, and an attempt to explain these changes. Lastly, it involves a confrontation between the ideas of equality and social hierarchy. Is equality an attainable ideal in the circumstances of a complex industrial society? And conversely, what kinds and degrees of inequality are inescapable, tolerable, or even desirable, in such a society?

The inequalities of social class should not be regarded as identical with human inequality in general. There are other forms of inequality, other kinds of privilege and domination, besides those which arise from differences of social class. Within particular societies there may be inequalities originating in differences of race, language or religion; and between societies there exist inequalities such as those so evident today between rich and poor nations, which are the outcome of conquest, of differences in size and natural resources, and of specific historical opportunities and failures. Nor are political rights always determined by class membership, as Marxists sometimes assert. Political power itself may create new social classes, new property rights, new privileges.

It remains true, none the less, that the division of society into distinct social classes is one of the most striking manifestations of inequality in the modern world, that it has often been the source of other kinds of inequality, and that the economic dominance of a particular class has very often been the basis for its political rule. Class, therefore, is deeply involved in many of the most vital questions of modern politics and social policy.

The Nature of Social Class

There is still much controversy among sociologists about the theory of social class, and more broadly, of social stratification. The latter term may be used to refer to any hierarchial ordering of social groups or strata in a society; and sociologists have generally distinguished its principal forms as being those of caste, estate, social class, and status group. Each of these types of social stratification is complex, and there are many unsettled questions about the basis and characteristics of castes and estates, just as there are about classes and status groups[1]; even though the former are more easily defined, and their boundaries more clearly distinguishable, in most cases. In spite of these difficulties, there are some general features of social stratification which are not in dispute.

In the first place, a system of ranks does not form part of some natural and invariable order of things, but is a human contrivance or product, and is subject to historical changes. More particularly, natural or biological inequalities, on one side, and the distinctions of social rank on the other, belong to two distinct orders of fact. The differences were pointed out very clearly by Rousseau in a well-known passage : 'I conceive that there are two kinds of inequality among the human species; one, which I call natural or physical, because it is established by nature, and consists in a difference of age, health, bodily strength, and the qualities of the mind or of the soul; and another, which may be called moral or political inequality, because it depends on a kind of convention, and is established, or at least authorized, by the consent of men. This latter consists of the different privileges, which some men enjoy to the

[1] See, for an excellent review of recent studies of caste, M.N. Srinivas *et al.* 'Caste', *Current Sociology*, Vol. VIII (3), 1959; and on the social hierarchy in feudal societies, Marc Bloch, *Feudal Society* (English trans., London 1961), Part VI.

prejudice of others; such as that of being more rich, more honoured, more powerful, or even in a position to exact obedience.'[2]

The distinction has been recognized by most modern writers on social class. Thus T.H. Marshall has observed that '. . . the institution of class teaches the members of a society to notice some differences and to ignore others when arranging persons in order of social merit.'[3] It might be argued, however, while accepting this distinction, that the social class system in modern capitalist societies does actually operate in such a way as to ensure a rough correspondence between the hierarchy of natural abilities and the socially recognized distinctions of rank. Such arguments have often been put forward,[4] but they are not well supported by the facts. It is generally admitted that the inequality of incomes is one important element in the class hierarchy. But numerous investigations have established that the inequality of incomes depends very largely upon the inequal distribution of property through inheritance, and not primarily upon the differences in earned income which might be supposed to have some connection with natural, or innate, abilities.[5] Modern studies of educational and occupational selection underline this lack of correspondence between the hierarchies of ability and of social position, inasmuch as they make clear that intellectual ability, for example, is by no means always rewarded with high income or high social status, nor lack of ability with the opposite. Indeed, it would be a more accurate description of the social class system to say that it operates, largely through the inheritance of property, to ensure that each individual maintains a certain social position, determined by his birth and irrespective of his particular abilities. This state of affairs is only mitigated, not abolished, by various social influences which we shall consider later.

A second point of general agreement is that social classes,

[2] J.J. Rousseau, *A Dissertation on the Origin and Foundation of the Inequality of Mankind,* Everyman edition, p. 160.

[3] T.H. Marshall, 'The Nature of Class Conflict' in *Citizenship and Social Class* (1950) p. 115.

[4] They are to be found especially in the *élite* theories of Pareto and Mosca which I have criticized in my *Elites and Society* (1964).

[5] See, for instance, H. Dalton, *Some Aspects of the Inequality of Incomes in Modern Societies* (1920).

in contrast with castes or feudal estates, are more exclusively economic groups. They are not constituted or supported by any specific legal or religious rules, and membership of a particular class confers upon the individual no special civil or political rights. It follows from this that the boundaries of social classes are less precisely defined. The principal classes, the *bourgeoisie* and the working class, may be fairly easily identifiable in most societies, but there are many intermediate strata, conveniently referred to as the 'middle classes', the boundaries of which are difficult to state exactly, and membership in which cannot be determined in any simple fashion.

Furthermore, the membership of modern social classes is usually less stable than that of other types of hierarchical group. The individual is born into a particular social class, just as he is born into a caste or estate, but he is somewhat less likely to remain at the social level in which he was born than is the individual in a caste or estate society. Within his own lifetime an individual, or his family, may rise or fall in the social hierarchy. If he rises, he needs no patent of nobility, no kind of official recognition, to confirm his new status. It will be enough for him to be wealthy, to have a particular economic and occupational role, and perhaps to acquire some of the secondary cultural characteristics of the social stratum into which he has moved.

Although the economic basis of social classes is obvious, the fact may be interpreted in various ways, which give rise to widely differing views of the significance of classes in social life and of the relations between classes. It will be useful to begin by examining Marx's interpretation, because it affirms so strongly the economic basis of classes and the antagonistic relations between them, and because a critical study of Marx's conception will reveal most of the vital problems concerning the nature of social classes.

Marx never set down a full and systematic account of his theory of class, although it may reasonably be said (as Lenin remarked) that everything he wrote was in some way concerned with the question of class. The point at which Marx began a connected exposition of his theory is just where the manuscript of the third volume of *Capital* breaks off unfinished, after one page in which he had set out mainly the difficulties which confronted his own theory. In fact, Marx first of all adopted a notion of class which was widely employed by historians and social theorists (including the early socialists) at the time when he began his sociological inquiries, and he was then largely concerned to fit this notion into the wider framework of his theory of social change, and to use it in analysing the development of one particular social system, namely modern capitalism. He indicated this himself when he wrote, in an early letter, '. . . no credit is due to me for discovering the existence of classes in modern society, nor yet the struggle between them. Long before me *bourgeois* historians had described the historical development of this struggle of the classes and *bourgeois* economists the economic anatomy of the classes.'[6] Marx went on to explain his own contribution as having been to show that the existence of classes is bound up with particular historical phases in the development of production, and that the conflict of classes in the modern capitalist societies will lead to the victory of the working class and to the inauguration of a classless, socialist society.

The distinctive features of Marx's theory are, therefore, the conception of social classes in terms of the system of production, and the idea of social development through class conflict which is to culminate in a new type of society without classes. As Marx saw it, '. . . the whole of what is called world history is nothing but the creation of man himself by human labour.'[7] Man produces (and reproduces) himself in a physical and in a cultural sense. 'In the social production which men carry on, they enter into definite relations that are indispensable and independent of their will; these relations of production correspond to a definite stage of development of their material powers of production. The totality of these relations of production constitutes the economic structure of society—the real foundation upon which legal and political superstructures arise and to which definite forms of social consciousness correspond. The mode of production of material life determines the general character of the social, political and spiritual processes of life.'[8]

[6] Letter to J. Weydemeyer, March 5, 1852.
[7] *Economic and Philosophical Manuscripts* (1844).
[8] *Contribution to the Critique of Political Economy* (1859). Preface.

Social classes originated with the first historical expansion of productive forces beyond the level needed for mere subsistence, involving the extension of the division of labour outside the family, the accumulation of surplus wealth, and the emergence of private ownership of economic resources. Thereafter, it is the differing relations of individuals to the privately owned instruments of production which form the basis for the constitution of social classes. Marx distinguished several important epochs, or major forms of social structure, in the history of mankind. In the preface to his *Contribution to the Critique of Political Economy* he writes : 'In broad outline we can designate the Asiatic, the ancient, the feudal, and the modern *bourgeois* modes of production as epochs in the progress of the economic formation of society.' Elsewhere, he and Engels refer to primitive communism, ancient society (slavery), feudal society (serfdom), and modern capitalism (wage labour) as the principal historical forms of society. Marx's references to the Asiatic type of society are especially interesting because this lies outside the line of development of the Western societies, and also because he seems to accept the possibility that in this case a ruling class might be formed by the high officials who control the administration.[9] But this theme was not pursued in his later work.

The historical changes from one type of society to another are brought about by class struggles and by the victory of one class over others. Class conflict itself reflects the incompatibility between different modes of production; and the victory of a

[9] See, on this question, the interesting essay by George Lichtheim, 'Marx and the "Asiatic Mode of Production" ', *St Anthony's Studies* No. 14 (1963). See also Marx's observations on pre-capitalist societies, taken from his preparatory manuscripts for *Capital*, in Karl Marx, *Pre-Capitalist Economic Formations,* edited by E.J. Hobsbawm (1964). Hobsbawm, in his introduction, argues that these texts show that Marx was not attempting to set out a general evolutionary scheme; but while it may be accepted that Marx was not an evolutionist in the grand manner of Comte or Spencer, it is to exaggerate in the opposite direction to claim that he had no evolutionary scheme at all in mind. There are several problems which Marx failed to resolve clearly in his writings; and one of them is precisely the question whether the transition from feudalism to capitalism, and the development of capitalist society, were to be regarded as special cases, or whether, and in what manner, they could be incorporated in a general account of the development of human society from its beginnings.

particular class, as well as its subsequent reorganization of society, is conditional upon the emergence of a new and superior mode of production, which it is the interest of this class to establish as dominant. In Marx's words : 'No social order ever disappears before all the productive forces for which there is room in it have been developed; and new, higher relations of production never appear before the material conditions of their existence have matured in the womb of the old society.'[10]

Marx was not, however, expounding a simple theory of technological or economic determinism. On the contrary, as he asserted in his criticism of Hegel's philosophy of history : 'It is not "history" which uses men as a means of achieving—as if it were an individual person—*its* own ends. History is *nothing* but the activity of men in pursuit of their ends.'[11] Marx held very strongly (and his own intellectual and political activities would otherwise have been absurd) that the victory of a rising class depends upon its awareness of its situation and aims, and upon the effectiveness of its political organization, as well as upon its actual economic position. This is especially the case with the working class in capitalist society, and Marx discussed on several occasions the factors which might influence the development of its class consciousness and of its political maturity. In *The Poverty of Philosophy*, for example, he examines at some length the development of the working class, and adds some critical remarks on the lack of empirical studies devoted to this most significant social movement : 'Many researches have been undertaken to trace the historical stages through which the *bourgeoisie* passed, from the commune up to its constitution as a class. But when it is a question of gaining a clear understanding of the strikes, combinations, and other forms in which the proletarians are achieving, before our eyes, their organization as a class, some are seized with genuine fear, while others display a transcendental disdain.' It is one of the most important features of Marx's theory of class, therefore, that it attempts to take account of the interplay between the real situation of individuals in the process of production, on

---

[10] *Contribution to the Critique of political Economy.* Preface.
[11] *The Holy Family* (1845).

one side, and the conceptions which they form of their situation and of the lines of social and political action which are open to them, on the other; and in its application to modern societies the theory allows a very great influence to ideas and doctrines. Marx's conviction that the working class would be victorious within a relatively short space of time in its struggle against the *bourgeoisie* was founded largely upon his conclusion that modern large-scale factory production would be extremely favourable to the development of class consciousness, to the diffusion of socialist ideas, and to the organization of a political movement.

Like other nineteenth-century thinkers who contributed to the foundation of sociology, Marx was particularly concerned to investigate the origins and development of modern capitalist society, and he chose to do so largely in a single country— England—because it was at that time the most advanced industrial country, showing to others, as Marx claimed, 'the image of their own future'. In its application to this English society of the mid-nineteenth century Marx's theory was extremely convincing. The course of industrial development seemed to confirm the thesis that society was becoming more clearly divided into two principal classes, a small class of increasingly wealthy capitalists and a growing mass of propertyless and impoverished wage-earners; and that the social gulf between them was widening as a result of the decline of the middle classes (by which Marx meant the small independent producers and independent professional men), whose members were being transformed into dependent employees. At the same time, the rise of the labour movement (of trade unions, co-operatives, and socialist political parties) and the outbreak of revolutionary conflicts all over Europe, especially in the years preceding 1848, provided evidence for Marx's prediction of a growth of class consciousness in the working class, and its expression in new social doctrines and new forms of political organization.

For the past eighty years Marx's theory has been the object of unrelenting criticism and of tenacious defence. These have concerned themselves with three principal aspects of the theory. First, there is the criticism which questions the pre-eminence that Marx assigned to social classes and class conflicts in explaining the major historical changes in human society. As a result of his preoccupation with class, it is said, Marx neglected other important social relationships, and in particular those which bind men together in national communities. This distorted his account of social change in two ways. It led him to underestimate the influence of nationalism and of conflict between nations in human history; an excusable error, perhaps, in the mid-nineteenth century, when Comte and Spencer, for example, both considered that warfare was likely to disappear altogether from human affairs. The growth of nationalist and imperialist sentiments during the latter part of the nineteenth century constitutes a particular problem for Marx's own theory, for although it can be interpreted as a diffusion of ruling class ideas the question remains as to why such ideas and sentiments were able to influence such a large part of the population at a time when the working class movement was growing vigorously and when Marxist doctrines were already widely known.

Marx also took little account of another aspect of the growing sense of national community in the European nations, which restrained and moderated the development of class antagonisms. In the mid-nineteenth century it was easy to distinguish the 'two nations' within each society; one of them participating fully and actively in, and directing, national affairs, while the other constituted only the raw material of policy. It was easy, too, to discern the massive movement of revolt which was taking shape among the members of this submerged and oppressed 'nation'. Yet even in Marx's lifetime there had begun the extension of political and social rights to new groups in the population, which has continued more rapidly in the twentieth century, and which has altered the relations between classes. New moral and social conceptions which emphasize common human interests within the nation, and the idea of 'citizenship', have been in part a cause, in part a consequence, of these changes.

The failure of class antagonisms in the industrial countries to attain that degree of intensity which Marx had anticipated, was shown most dramatically in 1914, when the European socialist parties, many of them Marxist in doctrine, supported almost unanimously the war waged by their own governments.

The same phenomenon is, however, revealed in a less dramatic way by the changes in working class politics during the twentieth century from revolutionary to reformist ideas and actions. In this process, it may be claimed, the social bond of nationality has proved more effective in creating a community than has that of class.

A second theme in the criticism of Marx has been that although his theory fits reasonably well the phenomena of class relations in modern capitalist societies, it does not fit so well, nor has it been used so successfully in explaining, a number of other types of social stratification. There are, in fact, in Marx's theory, two distinct uses of the term 'class' which illustrate this difficulty.[12] Very often—as in the famous opening passage of the *Communist Manifesto*, which begins : 'The history of all hitherto existing society is the history of class struggles'—Marx employs the term 'class' to refer to the major social groups—oppressors and oppressed—which are in conflict with each other in every type of human society beyond the most primitive. Elsewhere, however, Marx recognizes the distinctive features of modern social classes. In *The German Ideology*, he contrasts a class system with a system of estates, and observes : 'The distinction between the personal and the class individual, the accidental nature of conditions of life for the individual, appears only with the emergence of class, which itself is a product of the *bourgeoisie*.' Marx devoted himself largely to studying 'class' in this second sense, as his scientific works make abundantly clear, and so he did not have to confront in detail the difficulties which arise when his general theory of class is used to explain the origins and development of feudal societies, of a caste system, or of the Asiatic form of society which he had himself distinguished and briefly portrayed. The criticism here is not that Marx himself failed to test his theory in a sufficiently comprehensive way. He had formulated a new and exciting hypothesis, and had sought to test it rigorously in the case which he considered most significant from a theoretical and practical point of view; namely, the development of modern capitalism. The failure is that of

[12] The best account of the different conceptions of class which Marx brought together in his theory will be found in S. Ossowski, *Class Structure in the Social Consciousness* (London, 1963) Chapter V.

later Marxists, who have for the most part abstained from examining the usefulness and limitations of the theory when
applied to other historical situations.

The third line of criticism, which most nearly concerns us
here, attacks directly Marx's account of the development of
social classes in the modern capitalist societies. In broad outline, Marx predicted that the social gulf between the two principal classes, *bourgeoisie* and proletariat, would become wider,
in part because of the increasing disparity between their conditions of life,[18] and in part because of the elimination of the
intermediate strata of the population; that the class consciousness of the proletariat would develop and would assume a
revolutionary character; and that the rule of the bourgeoisie
would finally be overthrown by a revolution of the immense
majority of the population.

Against this view numerous arguments have been presented,
based upon sociological observation of the changes in the structure of modern societies. It is claimed, in the first place, that the
gulf between *bourgeoisie* and proletariat has not widened, for
several reasons. The productivity of modern industry, especially in the last few decades, has increased so greatly as to produce a considerable improvement in the general level of living;
and even if the distribution of income between the classes had
remained unchanged this would still have raised the working
class level of living to a point at which new aspirations and
new social attitudes would be encouraged, far removed from
those which support revolutionary aims. It is argued further,
however, that the distribution of national income has actually
changed in favour of the working class, thus reinforcing these
tendencies. The extent of the redistribution of income and
wealth in modern societies is a subject of controversy, and some
of the relevant studies will be considered in the next chapter;
but even a modest redistribution, together with the general rise
in incomes, the expansion of social services, and greater secur-

---

[18] Contrary to a popular belief Marx did not assert that the material
level of living of the working class must decline absolutely with the development of capitalism; his principal argument was that it would decline
relative to that of the *bourgeoisie,* either by remaining stationary while the
latter rose, or by rising less rapidly. See his brief exposition in *Wage-Labour
and Capital.*

ity of employment, would clearly bring about an important change in the position of the working class in society. It seems no longer possible in this second half of the twentieth century to regard the working class in the advanced industrial countries as being totally alienated from society, or, in Marx's phrase, as 'a class *in* civil society which is not a class *of* civil society'.

Another change which presents difficulties for Marx's theory is the growth of the 'new middle classes'. This does not directly falsify Marx's statement that the 'middle classes' would gradually disappear in modern societies, because he was referring to the large numbers of small producers, craftsmen, artisans, small farmers, self-employed professional men, many of whom have in fact been absorbed as paid employees into large capitalist enterprises. Nevertheless, it does contradict one of Marx's fundamental arguments, which was that the 'intermediate strata' would disappear, and that a simplified class structure of two clearly defined major classes would emerge. In the *Communist Manifesto* he wrote : 'Our epoch, the epoch of *bourgeoisie*, possesses, however, this distinctive feature; it has simplified the class antagonisms. Society as a whole is more and more splitting up into two great hostile camps, into two great classes directly facing each other—*bourgeoisie* and proletariat.'

The growth of the new middle classes—comprising office workers, supervisors, managers, technicians, scientists, and many of those who are employed in providing services of one kind or another (e.g. social welfare, entertainment, leisure activities)—which has resulted from economic development, manifests the greater complexity of social stratification in modern industrial societies, and it introduces, or re-introduces, as an important element of stratification, social prestige based upon occupation, consumption and style of life. Max Weber, who was the first to present a comprehensive alternative to Marx's theory, did so by distinguishing, in the first place, between different modes of stratification which coexisted in modern societies : class stratification, with which Marx had been primarily concerned, and stratification by social prestige or honour. He also treated as an independent phenomenon the distribution of political power in society, which Marx had viewed almost exclusively as the product of class stratification. In Weber's conception it is clear that stratification by prestige, which gives rise to the formation of status groups, is regarded as having its source in those pre-capitalist groups which enjoyed social honour, such as the various sections of the nobility, the scholarly professions, and the high officials; but the new middle classes in the advanced industrial societies exhibit some at least of the same features in basing their claims to social position upon educational and cultural characteristics, upon the nature of their occupations, and upon their particular styles of life.

Stratification by prestige affects the class system, as Marx conceived it, in two important ways : first, by interposing between the two major classes a range of status groups which bridge the gulf between the extreme positions in the class structure; and secondly, by suggesting an entirely different conception of the social hierarchy as a whole, according to which it appears as a continuum of more or less clearly defined status positions, determined by a variety of factors and not simply by property ownership, which is incompatible with the formation of massive social classes and with the existence of a fundamental conflict between classes. The relations between status groups at different levels are relations of competition and emulation, not of conflict. With the growth in numbers of the middle classes, which form an increasing proportion of the whole population, this view of the social hierarchy as a continuum of prestige ranks (or statuses), without any sharp breaks, and thus without any clear lines of conflict between major social groups, has acquired a much greater influence upon social thought and its diffusion has served to check the growth of class consciousness. Consequently, whereas Max Weber regarded class stratification and status stratification as co-existing in modern societies, their relative importance fluctuating with changes in technology and economic conditions, some recent sociologists have concluded that status groups have now become far more important than social classes in the system of stratification as a whole.

This conclusion is supported by two other arguments. One of them asserts that the amount of social mobility in industrial societies is so considerable as to prevent the consolidation and persistence of classes in Marx's sense, and that, on the contrary, it too makes plausible the image of the social hierarchy as a series of levels of prestige, as a ladder with closely adjacent rungs, which individuals may climb or descend according to their capacities.[14] However, the amount and range of social mobility, like the distribution of income, have been assessed in conflicting ways, and some of the evidence from recent studies will be considered later.

A second argument, which derives ultimately from Weber's distinction between class stratification and the distribution of political power, has been set out most forcefully by R. Dahrendorf, in his *Class and Class Conflict in Industrial Society*. Dahrendorf's main thesis is that the coincidence of economic conflict and political conflict, which was the foundation of Marx's theory, has ceased to exist in what he terms the 'post-capitalist societies'. In capitalist society, Dahrendorf argues : '. . . the lines of industrial and political conflict were superimposed. The opponents of industry—capital and labour—met again, as *bourgeoisie* and proletariat, in the political arena. . . It is one of the central theses of the present analysis that in post-capitalist society, industry and society have, by contrast to capitalist society, been dissociated. Increasingly, the social relations of industry, including industrial conflict, do not dominate the whole of society but remain confined in their patterns and problems to the sphere of industry. Industry and industrial conflict are, in post-capitalist society, institutionally isolated, i.e. confined within the borders of their proper realm and robbed of their influence on other spheres of society.' (op. cit. p. 268). Considered empirically, however, these propositions are more easily falsified than those of Marx which they are intended to replace; for numerous studies have shown that in the European industrial countries, and to a lesser extent in the USA, the major political conflicts are closely and continuously associated with industrial conflicts, and express the divergent interests of the principal social classes. Dahrendorf's criticisms of Marx's theory are more plausible in their less extreme formulations; as for example, that there are other con-

---

[14] This view is implied in the functionalist theory of social stratification presented by K. Davis and W.E. Moore in their article 'Some principles of stratification', *American Sociological Review*, April, 1945; and also, to some extent, in S.M. Lipset's and R. Bendix's *Social Mobility in Industrial Society* Berkeley 1959).

flict groups in society besides social classes, which may at times assume great importance, that the association between industrial conflict and political conflict cannot simply be taken for granted, but must be investigated in each case, and that, with the development of the capitalist industrial societies, some significant changes have occurred in the nature of political conflicts themselves which could not be clearly foreseen or taken into account by Marx.

Besides the kind of criticism we have just considered, which questions Marx's account of the relations between classes, there is another which disputes the validity of his analysis of the principal classes—*bourgeoisie* and proletariat—in view of the changes which they have undergone during the twentieth century. The *bourgeoisie*, it is argued, is no longer a closed, cohesive and enduring group. Its structure, its composition, and its stability over time, have all been profoundly modified by the wider diffusion of property ownership and the break-up of large fortunes, by increasing social mobility, and by other changes in society. Furthermore, it can no longer be maintained that the *bourgeoisie* is a *ruling* class; first, because it has ceased to be a cohesive group; secondly, because the complexity and differentiation of modern societies make it difficult for any single group to wield power alone; and finally, because universal suffrage ensures that political power is ultimately in the hands of the mass of the people.

The changes in the condition of the working class appear even more damaging to Marx's theory. Marx expected the working class to become more homogeneous, because differences of skill and earnings would be reduced, if not obliterated, by the more extensive use of machinery; to become numerically stronger, because many members of the old middle class would sink to the condition of wage-earners; to become more united and class conscious as a result of the increasing similarity of conditions of life and work, the facility of communication among working class organizations, and the spread of socialist doctrines; and finally, to become a revolutionary force, because of the growing disparity between its own material conditions and those of the *bourgeoisie*, and the realization that only a radical transformation of society could make possible a tolerable human life for the great majority of men. Against this conception, the critics have pointed out that the modern working class remains highly differentiated in respect of levels of skill, even though differences in earnings have tended to diminish; that increasing specialization of occupations has created a far more complex status system, as well as a multiplicity of sectional interests; that the expansion of the middle classes has reduced the proportion of industrial workers in the total population and thereby diminished their social influence; that greater social mobility has undermined the solidarity of the working class; and that the general improvement in levels of living has led to the *embourgeoisement* of the working class as a whole, which is now adopting middle class standards and patterns of life.

Some part of this criticism has certainly to be accepted in any realistic account of the working class in present-day industrial societies, but the changes which have taken place are still open to various interpretations. The most disputed thesis is that concerning the *embourgeoisement* of the working class, which has often been presented in a superficial and facile manner. It has only recently been examined carefully by Goldthorpe and Lockwood,[15] who observe that as a result of recent studies of British society '. . . a picture has been built up—and it is one which would be generally accepted—of a system of stratification becoming increasingly fine in its gradations and at the same time somewhat less extreme and less rigid. Of late, however, still further economic progress has resulted in a new factor entering into the discussion—that of working class "affluence". . . It has been argued by a number of writers that the working class, or at least a more prosperous section of it, is losing its identity as a social stratum and is becoming merged into the middle class. . . This, one should note, is to claim a far more rapid and far-reaching change in class structure than any which could ensue from secular trends in occupational distribution, in the overall distribution of income and wealth or in rates of intergenerational social mobility.' The authors then distinguish and examine what they call the economic, the relational and the normative aspects of the changes in working class life. They point out that the economic progress of the working class in relation to the middle class has been exaggerated in many studies, because these do not take account of all the relevant factors, such as economic security, opportunities for promotion, and fringe benefits of various kinds. The other aspects, the relational (i.e. the extent to which manual workers are accepted on terms of equality by middle class people in formal and informal social relationships), and the normative (i.e. the extent to which manual workers have acquired a new outlook and new standards of behaviour which resemble those of the middle class), have hardly been studied at all; but such evidence as there is suggests that the gulf between working class and middle class remains very wide. It follows that the political conclusions—the end of ideology and of class conflict—drawn from the so-called *embourgeoisement* of the working class, or in other words, from the view that the modern industrial countries are now middle class societies, are themselves extremely dubious.

A recent French study, by Serge Mallet,[16] points to some conclusions which supplement those reached by Goldthorpe and Lockwood. Mallet makes an important distinction between the situation of the worker in the spheres of consumption and of production. In the former, 'the working class has ceased to live apart. Its level of living and its aspirations for material comfort have led it out of the ghetto in which it was confined at the beginning of industrialization. The worker ceases to regard himself as a worker when he leaves the factory.' In the process of production itself, on the contrary, 'the fundamental characteristics which distinguish the working class from other social strata seem to have remained unchanged'.[17] It is in industry, through the factory organizations and the trade unions, that the distinctive characteristics and outlook of the working class are maintained or changed; and Mallet argues, from his studies of three industrial enterprises, that the 'new working class' has been led, as a result of technological and economic changes, to assume greater responsibility for the organization of production, through its trade union represent-

[16] Serge Mallet, *La nouvelle classe ouvrière* (Paris, 1963).
[17] op. cit. p. 9.

atives, and thus to see itself still, and perhaps even more clearly, as the eventual controller of industry in place of the present capitalist owners.

We have lastly to consider a criticism of Marx's theory which arises directly from the social and political experiences of the Soviet-type countries. It is best expressed in the words of a Polish sociologist, the late Stanislaw Ossowski : 'There are other reasons why the nineteenth-century conception of social class, in both the liberal and the Marxian interpretations, has lost much of its applicability in the modern world. In situations where changes of social structure are to a greater or lesser extent governed by the decision of the political authorities, we are a long way from social class as interpreted by Marx, Ward, Veblen or Weber, from classes conceived of as groups determined by their relations to the means of production or, as others would say, by their relations to the market. We are a long way from classes conceived of as groups arising out of the spontaneously created class organizations. In situations where the political authorities can overtly and effectively change the class structure; where the privileges that are most essential for social status, including that of a higher share in the national income, are conferred by a decision of the political authorities; where a large part or even the majority of the population is included in a stratification of the type to be found in a bureaucratic hierarchy—the nineteenth-century concept of class becomes more or less an anachronism, and class conflicts give way to other forms of social antagonism.'[18] This is most clearly apposite to the USSR, and to societies of the same type, in which the rule of a single party, unchecked by any organized opposition, has allowed an authoritarian ordering of income and rank in a highly inegalitarian system; but it also has some relevance to the modern capitalist societies, in which the state has acquired a degree of independence from social classes and is now a source of changes in stratification through its own social legislation.

Neither of these instances can be comprehended by the Marxist theory in its most rigorous form. Marx did not foresee either that the dictatorship of the proletariat as he conceived

[18] S. Ossowski, *Class Structure in the Social Consciousness*, p. 184.

it would actually appear as the dictatorship of a party, and eventually as a bureaucratic régime controlled by a single individual, or that in the capitalist countries the working class movement itself would help to bring about a form of society, the Welfare State, which may be transitional or enduring, which is not socialist, but in which there is a substantial control by government over the economy and social conditions, and a corresponding influence upon the system of stratification.

The criticisms of Marx's theory, and the alternative views which have been put forward, based mainly upon Max Weber's distinction between class stratification and stratification by prestige, do not amount as yet to a comprehensive new theory, which can take the place of that which Marx proposed. They provide, rather, a more or less systematic inventory of the outstanding problems—the nature of social stratification in the Soviet societies, and of its modifications in the capitalist societies; the relative importance of property ownership, educational selection, occupational differentiation, and political power, in creating and maintaining social distinctions; the extent and consequences of social mobility and of income inequalities—and a conceptual scheme which attempts to draw more careful distinctions between social classes, status groups and *élites*, and between the economic, the political and other elements in social stratification. The value of these new concepts and of the critical revisions of Marx's theory, can be better assessed if we now make use of them in an examination of the changes which have taken place in the class structure of some modern societies.

Classes in the Industrial Societies

The two broad types of industrial society which I distinguished earlier—capitalist and Soviet—present a number of similar features in their occupational structure and in the general shape of their social stratification, but they also differ widely in their political régimes and their social doctrines and policies, in the manner in which the upper social strata are constituted, and in the historical changes of social structure which they have undergone. It is desirable, therefore, to begin by examining each type of society separately, before attempting any comparison.

In the mid-nineteenth century England was generally regarded as showing most fully and clearly the typical class structure of the new capitalist society. Marx chose England as his model for studying the development of capitalism and the formation of the principal modern classes—*bourgeoisie* and proletariat—although he associated with this a model of class conflict and revolution which he derived mainly from the experiences of France. Disraeli, who was not a revolutionary, documented in *Sybil* and in other writings the formation of 'two nations' within English society, warned against the dangers springing from this rift between the manufacturers and the industrial workers, and at the same time sought to turn it to advantage by enlisting the support of working men for the Tory party against the Liberals. The English class system had, however, some peculiar features which arose according to R.H. Tawney, from 'the blend of a crude plutocratic reality with the sentimental aroma of an aristocratic legend'.[1] It was this set of circumstances—still to be exhaustively studied and explained by historians—which created in England the 'gentleman ideal' and the public schools as agencies for con-

[1] R.H. Tawney, *Equality* (4th edn. 1952) p. 57.

solidating and transmitting it. It produced also the snobbery of the middle classes, the 'religion of inequality' as Matthew Arnold called it, which maintained fine but strict social distinctions at which foreign observers marvelled.

What changes has this system undergone in the past century? The plutocratic reality, it may be said, has been altered by changes in the distribution of property and income, and above all by the general improvement in the levels of living. At the end of the nineteenth century severe poverty was still widespread. Charles Booth's survey of London,[2] carried out between 1887 and 1891, showed that at that time more than 30 per cent of the inhabitants were living in poverty; and similar conclusions emerged from Rowntree's study of social conditions in York,[3] begun in 1899. At the other end of the social hierarchy, in the years 1911–13, a privileged 1 per cent of the population owned 68 per cent of all private property and received 29 per cent of the total national income.

The attack upon economic inequality is of very recent date. An estate duty was first imposed towards the end of the nineteenth century, and only in 1949 did it reach the substantial rate of 80 per cent on estates above £1 million. Even so, these rates of taxation reduce large fortunes (and the resulting unearned incomes) very slowly, if at all, since they are counteracted by various forms of tax avoidance, and by capital gains in periods of economic expansion, which can quickly restore fortunes diminished by taxation as well as creating new ones. In 1946–7, 1 per cent of the population still owned 50 per cent of all private property, and it is unlikely that the proportion has changed very much since then. The traditional wealthy class has obviously retained most of its wealth. As Anthony Sampson has observed : '. . . the aristocracy are, in general, much richer than they seem. With democracy has come discretion. Their London palaces and outward show have disappeared, but the countryside is still full of millionaire peers : many of them, with the boom in property, are richer now than they have ever been.'[4] The observation is probably just as true of wealthy financial or manufacturing families.

[2] Charles Booth, *Life and Labour of the People in London* (1902).
[3] B. Seebohm Rowntree, *Poverty; A Study of Town Life* (1901).
[4] Anthony Sampson, *Anatomy of Britain*, pp. 4–5.

The distribution of income is affected by several factors other than the distribution of wealth—by the state of employment, collective bargaining, general social policy, and taxation. During the present century taxes upon income have been used increasingly in attempts to bring about a redistribution between rich and poor; and whereas in 1913 those with earned incomes of £10,000 a year or above paid only about 8 per cent of their income in direct taxation, in 1948 those in the same category paid 75 per cent or more in direct taxation. R.H. Tawney, in the epilogue to the 1952 edition of his *Equality*, noted that the number of incomes exceeding £6,000 a year after payment of tax had declined to a very small figure, and that whereas in 1938 the average retained income of those in the highest category (£10,000 a year and above) was twenty-eight times as great as the income of those in the lowest category (£250–£499 a year), in 1948 it was only thirteen times as great.

However, the tax returns do not provide anything like a complete picture of the distribution of income, and R.M. Titmuss, in the most thorough study of the question which has yet been made,[5] points to the influence of life assurances, superannuation, tax-free payments on retirement, education covenants, discretionary trusts, expense accounts, and capital gains, in conserving or increasing the wealth and income of the upper class. With the present inadequate data it is impossible to arrive at a precise statement of the changes in income distribution which have occurred during the twentieth century. Most students of the problem, however, have concluded that from 1900 to 1939 there was little or no redistribution of income in favour of wage-earners, and that at the end of the period some 10 per cent of the population received almost half the national income while the other 90 per cent of the population received the other half; that between 1939 and 1949 redistribution may have transferred some 10 per cent of the national income from property owners to wage earners; but that since 1949 there has again been growing inequality. These calculations are based largely upon the income tax returns, and so they do not take

[5] R.M. Titmuss, *Income Distribution and Social Change* (1962).

account of the other sources of real income mentioned above, which benefit mainly the rich.

Both Rowntree and Booth concluded from their investigations that two of the most important causes of poverty were the lack of regular employment and the expenses of protracted ill-health. The improvement in the conditions of life for the working class in postwar Britain obviously owes much to the maintenance of full employment and to the development of the health services.[6] Full employment, besides raising the level of income of the working class and providing a degree of that economic security which the upper class has always taken for granted, has almost entirely eliminated the class of domestic servants; and this is one of the greatest gains which the working class has made in the twentieth century, in escaping from one particularly onerous form of subjection to another class.[7]

It may be argued, too, that the social services as a whole have a much greater effect in diminishing class differences than would appear from their economic consequences alone. As R.H. Tawney wrote :

'There are certain gross and crushing disabilities—conditions of life injurious to health, inferior education, economic insecurity . . . which place the classes experiencing them at a permanent disadvantage with those not similarly afflicted. There are certain services by which these crucial disabilities have been greatly mitigated, and, given time and will, can be altogether removed . . . The contribution to equality made by these dynamic agencies is obviously out of all proportion greater than that which would result from an annual present to every individual among the forty odd millions concerned of a sum equivalent to his quota of the total cost.'[8]

---

[6] Rowntree emphasizes the importance of these factors in his third social survey of York. See B. Seebohm Rowntree and G.R. Lavers, *Poverty and the Welfare State* (1951).

[7] Marx observed in *Capital* Vol. I that the vast increase in the numbers of domestic servants, of whom there were well over a million in 1861, showed clearly the growing divergence between the classes; with wealth and luxury concentrated at one extreme, poverty and servitude at the other.

[8] R.H. Tawney, *Equality* (4th edn. 1952) p. 248.

The social services do not only help to create an equality in the vital conditions of life for all citizens; so far as they are used by everyone the standard of the service tends to rise. It may well be true, as some have argued, that the middle classes have benefited at least as much as the working class from the expansion of the social services, but one important consequence has been that, for example, the standards of free medical care have been vastly improved as compared with the time when such care was provided only for the poor and needy. In the field of education a similar progress is evident since the Education Act of 1944, although here class differences have proved more tenacious and difficult to overcome, while the existence of a large private sector of education has meant that there has been less vigour in the drive to improve the standard of the public service.

We must conclude that the general advance in the material conditions of the British working class, in recent decades, has been due overwhelmingly to the rapid growth of national income, which has also made possible the expansion of the social services, and not to any radical redistribution of wealth or income between classes. Moreover, even in this more affluent society a great deal of poverty remains. Its significance for the relations between classes is, however, very different from that which it had in the nineteenth century. Then, poverty was the lot of a whole class, and there was no expectation that it could be quickly alleviated within the limits of the capitalist economic system. It separated one class in society distinctly from others, and at the same time engendered a movement of revolt. In present day Britain, as in other advanced industrial countries, poverty has ceased to be of this kind; it is now less extensive, and is confined to particular groups in the population —mainly old people and workers in certain occupations or regions which have been left behind as a result of technological progress—which are too isolated or heterogeneous to form the basis of a radical social movement. These impoverished groups stand in marked contrast with the majority of the working class which enjoys a high level of living in relation both to past societies and to some middle class groups in present day society.

The thesis of *embourgeoisement*, which was briefly examined in the previous chapter, relies in the main for its factual basis upon this improvement in levels of living and the changes in the relative economic position of manual workers and some sections of white collar workers, but it also brings in the effects of social mobility in modifying the class system. Since the war, sociologists have studied social mobility much more intensively than they have studied the changes within classes themselves, and they have attributed much importance to it as a solvent of class divisions. The findings of recent studies[9] may be summarized in the following way. Social mobility has generally increased with the economic development of the industrial societies, but the increase has been due very largely to changes in the occupational structure; that is, to the expansion of white collar and professional occupations and the contraction of manual occupations. For this reason, S.M. Miller has suggested that sociologists ought to give more attention to 'downward mobility', which involves a real exchange of occupational and social position between classes and may well be '. . . a better indicator of fluidity in a society than is upward mobility.'[10]

A second important feature is that most social mobility takes place between social levels which are close together; for example, between the upper levels of the working class and the lower levels of the middle class. Movement from the working class into the upper class is very limited in any society, and notably so in Britain.[11] This characteristic can be shown more clearly by studies of recruitment to particular *élite* occupations such as the higher civil service, business management, and the older professions. In Britain, a study of the directors of large public companies reveals that more than half of them began their careers with the advantage of having business connections in the family, while another 40 per cent came from families of landowners, professional men and others of similar

[9] See especially, D.V. Glass (ed.), *Social Mobility in Britain* (1954). This comprehensive study, based mainly upon a national sample survey, has provided a model for a number of later investigations in other countries. For comparative studies which bring together much recent research see S.M. Lipset and R. Bendix, *Social Mobility in Industrial Society* (1959), and S.M. Miller, 'Comparative Social Mobility', *Current Sociology*, IX (1) 1960.

[10] S.M. Miller, op. cit. p. 59.

[11] S.M. Miller, op. cit. p. 40.

social position.[12] A study of higher civil servants in the administrative class shows that 30 per cent came from families of the upper and upper middle classes, and another 40 per cent from the intermediate levels of the middle class, while only 3 per cent were recruited from families of semi-skilled and unskilled manual workers.[13] Nevertheless, the same study indicates that the area of recruitment of high civil servants has been extended somewhat during the past 30 years, and the same may well be true in the case of other professions.

The main influence here has been the extension of educational opportunities; and the view that social mobility has increased substantially in postwar Britain derives very largely from the belief that educational reforms have provided vast new opportunities for upward movement. It is certainly true that before the war social mobility was restricted especially by financial and other obstacles in the way of access to secondary and higher education.[14] The Education Act of 1944 established for the first time a national system of secondary education and greatly increased the opportunities for working class children to obtain a grammar school education.[15] Also in the postwar period the access of working class children to university has been made somewhat easier by the increase of student numbers and the more lavish provision of maintenance grants. Nevertheless, Britain is still very far from having equality of opportunity in education. The existence of a private sector of school education, misleadingly called the 'public schools', maintains the educational and occupational advantages of upper class families, while in the state system of education, although the opportunities for working class children have increased, it is probable that middle class families have actually made greater use of the new opportunities for grammar school

[12] G.H. Copeman, *Leaders of British Industry; A Study of the Careers of More than a Thousand Public Company Directors* (1955).

[13] R.K. Kelsall, *Higher Civil Servants in Britain* (1955).

[14] See data presented in L. Hogben (ed.), *Political Arithmetic* (1938).

[15] D.V. Glass notes, in his introduction to *Social Mobility in Britain,* that in one region, S.W. Hertfordshire, between the 1930's and 1951, '. . . the proportion of children of manual workers in the total entry to grammar schools rose from about 15 per cent to 43 per cent.' See also the material given in J.E. Floud, A.H. Halsey and F.M. Martin, *Social Class and Educational Opportunity* (1956).

and university education.[16] Even if we add to the social mobility which takes place through the educational system, that which may be assumed to occur as a result of the growth of new middle class occupations—for example, in the entertainments industry—where educational qualifications are less important, it can still not be said that the movement of individuals in the social hierarchy is very considerable or is increasing rapidly. The vast majority of people still remain in their class of origin.

It may be questioned, too, whether even a much higher rate of social mobility, involving an interchange between classes in which downward mobility was roughly equal to upward mobility, would have much effect upon the class system, in the sense of reducing the barriers or the antagonism between classes. On the contrary, in such a situation of high mobility, the working class would come to comprise those who had failed to rise in the social hierarchy in spite of the opportunities available to them, and those who had descended, through personal failure, from higher social levels; and such a class, made up of particularly embittered and frustrated individuals, might be expected to be very sharply distinguished from, and in conflict with, the rest of society. There are apparent, indeed, in Britain and in other industrial societies, some elements of such a condition among the younger generations in the population.

The most important aspect of social mobility is perhaps the impression which it makes upon the public consciousness. According to the type and degree of social mobility a society may appear to its members to be 'open' and fluid, presenting manifold opportunities to talent and energy, or it may appear to be rigid and 'closed'. In Britain, all manner of ancient institutions and modes of behaviour—the aristocracy, the public schools, Oxbridge, differences of speech and accent, the relationships of the 'old boy' network—frustrate mobility and buttress the public conception of a rigidly hierarchical society. Any increase in social mobility, even in the past two decades, has been too modest, gradual and discreet to create a new out-

[16] Appendix Two (B) to the *Report on Higher Education* (Cmnd. 2154) observes that the proportion of university students coming from working class families remained almost unchanged (at about 25 per cent) between 1928–47 and 1961.

look. The boundaries of class may have become more blurred, chiefly at the lower levels of the social hierarchy and there may have been some expansion of opportunities, especially in the sphere of consumption, for large sections of the population. But there is no general sense of greater 'classlessness', nor of great opportunities for the individual to choose and create his way of life regardless of inherited wealth or social position.

It was in the general acceptance of an egalitarian ideology, which still persists in some degree, that the USA differed most remarkably from the European societies in the nineteenth century. In America, there was no established system of feudal ranks, no historical memory of an aristocratic order of society, which could provide a model for a new social hierarchy. The American war of independence indeed was an important influence upon the European revolutions against the *ancien régime*. In the USA, in contrast with the European countries, the ownership of property was quite widely diffused in the early part of the nineteenth century, and some 80 per cent of the working population (excluding the Negro slaves) owned the means of production with which they worked. America was, predominantly, a society of small farmers, small traders, and and small businessmen; the closest approach there has been to a 'property-owning democracy'. Of course, disparities of wealth existed, but they were not so extreme as in Europe, and they did not give rise, except in some of the southern states, to disparities of social rank comparable with those in the still aristocratic and oligarchical European societies. De Tocqueville saw in the USA the prime example of a tendency towards equality in modern societies; a society in which, as he wrote: 'Great wealth tends to disappear, the number of small fortunes to increase.'

The sense of belonging to a society of equals was enhanced by the possibility of easy movement in the still rudimentary hierarchy of wealth. America was the 'land of opportunity', a vast, unexplored and unexploited country in which it was always possible, or seemed possible, to escape from economic want or subjection by moving to a new place, acquiring land or some other property, and adding to it by personal effort and talent.

A century and a half of economic change has destroyed most of the foundations upon which the egalitarian ideology rested. The society made up of small property owners and independent producers began to be undermined soon after the civil war. The 1880's and 1890's, a period in which industry grew rapidly and modern communications were vastly expanded, saw the 'closing of the frontier', the emergence of the first industrial and financial trusts, and a considerable growth of inequalities of wealth. Class divisions began to appear more clearly, and to resemble more closely those in the European societies, and they were more openly asserted. The conscious emergence of an upper class was signalled by the establishment of the *Social Register* (the guide to the new American 'aristocracy'), and by the foundation of exclusive boarding schools and country clubs; and wealth and social position came increasingly to be transmitted through family connections. At the same time the working class became more strongly organized in trade unions and political associations, and from the 1890's to the 1930's there were numerous attempts, though without any lasting success, to bring these associations together in a broad socialist movement.

The changes in the economic system can be documented clearly from the statistics of occupations. Early in the nineteenth century 80 per cent of the employed white population were independent (self-employed) producers; by 1870 only 41 per cent were self-employed, and by 1940 only 18 per cent. In the words of C. Wright Mills:

'Over the last hundred years, the United States has been transformed from a nation of small capitalists into a nation of hired employees; but the ideology suitable for the nation of small capitalists persists, as if that small-propertied world were still a going concern.'[17]

There are several reasons for the persistence of this inapt ideology, apart from the inertia which characterizes social doctrines in general. One is that the concentration of property ownership was not accompanied by any sudden expansion of

[17] C. Wright Mills, *White Collar; The American Middle Classes* (1951).

the working class, or by any decline in the level of living. The industrial workers formed 28 per cent of the population in 1870, and 31 per cent in 1940; and wage-earners as a whole made up 53 per cent of the population in 1870, and 57 per cent in 1940. During the same period, however, the proportion of salaried employees in the population increased very rapidly, from 7 per cent to 25 per cent; and this expansion of the new white collar middle classes made possible a new kind of social mobility, in place of that which had been achieved earlier by the settlement of fresh lands.

Again, the concentration of wealth and income in a few hands seems never to have proceeded so far in America as in many European countries; and the gilded age of spectacular fortunes in the midst of widespread poverty lasted for a relatively short time. As in other industrial countries there has been a persistent effort to redistribute wealth and income in the USA through progressive taxation, estate duties, and taxes on capital gains. Since the war, the continued economic expansion, rising levels of living, and the steady growth of the middle classes, have had their effect upon the class structure in the same way as in other countries, but in a more conspicuous fashion. And whilst in Britain, for example, such changes have so far produced only modifications and questionings of a class system which is still extremely solid and which profoundly affects political life, in America they have brought instead confirmation of an inherited ideology of 'classlessness' and have practically extinguished the tentative class consciousness which found expression in the politics of the 1930's.

This divergence is not to be explained by a higher rate of social mobility in the USA in recent times, nor by a more rapid progress in the redistribution of wealth and income. Several studies have indicated that the USA does not have a rate of mobility significantly higher than that of some other industrial societies, in which class-consciousness is nevertheless much more intense.[18] This is the case, at least, when the broad movement from manual to non-manual occupations is considered. The long-range movement from the manual strata into the

[18] See especially, S.M. Lipset and R. Bendix, *Social Mobility in Industrial Society* (1959).

élites does seem to be greater in the USA than in most other countries;[19] but even so, it has not been very considerable at any time during the present century. W. Miller has shown that even in the first decade of the century successful businessmen had not generally risen from the lower strata of society, but had come for the most part from old-established families in the business and professional strata.[20] Similarly, a very thorough study of social classes in Philadelphia has revealed that the leading positions in the economic system are occupied predominantly by individuals from the established upper class families.[21]

The idea that a steady reduction of income inequalities has been proceeding during the present century is strongly contested, just as a similar view is contested in Britain. In the case of the USA the contention rests largely upon the statistical studies of national income by Simon Kuznets;[22] but as Gabriel Kolko has recently pointed out[23] the relevant part of these studies deals only with the wealthiest 5 per cent of the population, and does not examine the changes which have taken place in the incomes of other groups in the population. Kolko's own calculations, based upon studies of personal incomes before taxation by the National Industrial Conference Board (for 1910–37) and by the Survey Research Center (for 1941–59) indicate that between 1910 and 1959 the share in national income of the top income-tenth declined only slightly (and has fluctuated around 30 per cent in the past decade), while the shares of the second and third income-tenths actually increased and the shares of the two poorest income-tenths declined sharply (from 8.3 per cent of national income to only 4 per cent). Kolko also observes, as Titmuss has done in his study of the same question in Britain, that calculations based upon declarations of pre-tax income necessarily leave out of

[19] S.M. Miller, op. cit. p. 58.

[20] William Miller, 'American Historians and the Business Elite', in William Miller (ed.) *Men in Business* (new edn. 1962).

[21] E. Digby Baltzell, *An American Business Aristocracy* (new edn. 1962).

[22] See especially his *Shares of Upper Income Groups in Income and Savings* (1953).

[23] Gabriel Kolko, *Wealth and Power in America* (1962).

account various forms of real income which benefit mainly the upper class and thus increase inequality.

It may be argued, then, that it is the traditional conception of American society as highly mobile rather than any exceptional degree of mobility at the present time, and the general increase in prosperity (though with a good deal of partially concealed poverty)[24] rather than any strong movement towards greater economic equality, which play the main part in weakening class consciousness. But there have also been other factors at work, especially in inhibiting the development of a working class movement in which the ideas of class interest, and of socialism as an alternative form of society, would have a major influence. Among these factors, the situation of the Negroes and the successive waves of immigration are particularly important. The Negroes have formed a distinctive American proletariat, with the lowest incomes, the most menial and subservient tasks, and the lowest social prestige (in part because of their slave origins) of any group in American society. The existence of this large, relatively homogeneous, easily identifiable, and exploited group, has meant that every white American, even the lowest paid labourer, possesses a certain social prestige which raises him, at least in his own view, above the level of a proletarian. Immigration has worked in the same way to raise the social position of the ordinary American worker, since many groups of immigrants (the latest being the Puerto Ricans) entered the lowest levels of the occupational hierarchy, and made it possible for those already established to advance themselves. But neither the Negroes, nor any immigrant group, have formed a proletariat in the sense that they have challenged the established order of society. And so, although the present vigorous struggle of the Negroes to gain full economic, civil and political rights may be likened to early class conflicts in Europe so far as these were concerned with the right to vote, with labour legislation and with social reform,

[24] See, on the extent of poverty, Gunnar Myrdal, *Challenge to Affluence* (1963) Chapter 4, and Michael Harrington, *The Other America* (1962). The latter book makes plain that poverty is widespread, but (as in Britain) it is concentrated in particular sections of the population—here among the old, ethnic minorities, and workers in such regions as the Appalachians—and so often tends to go unrecognized.

it differs entirely from these conflicts in so far as it aims exclusively at winning acceptance in the existing society and accepts the predominant values of that society. The success of the struggles waged by Negroes and other ethnic minorities, however, would diminish the importance of ethnic divisions in American society, and one result might be the appearance of more sharply differentiated social classes and a greater awareness of class interests.

Against this development, however, there are working the same influences which we have seen in Britain : a more or less continuous rise in levels of living; a greater differentiation of the occupational structure, and so a more complex type of social stratification; a relative decline of manual occupations; and an expansion of educational opportunities which has already gone much farther in America than in other countries. These influences are at work in all the Western capitalist societies; in France, Germany and Italy, where, in the past, class divisions have been deeper and class conflicts more violent than in Britain, and equally in the Scandinavian countries, in which social welfare and equality of opportunity have advanced farther than elsewhere. The consequences are to be seen in a relative appeasement of bitter conflicts over the structure of society as a whole, and in a displacement of political interest towards new problems of technological advance, economic growth and modernization. The two cultures have replaced the two nations as a subject of political debate, at least for many Western intellectuals. Whether the changes in social conditions and attitudes have actually brought about, or will bring about, a consolidation of the present social structure in the Western countries, and what other political consequences they are likely to have, are questions which I shall consider later on.

Our immediate concern is to examine the evolution of classes in the Soviet type of industrial society. According to Marx's view modern capitalism would be 'the last antagonistic form of the process of production'. As he wrote in *The Poverty of Philosophy* :

'The condition for the emancipation of the working class is the abolition of all classes . . . The working class, in the course of its development, will substitute for the old civil society an association which will exclude classes and their antagonism.'

The USSR, although the revolution which created it did not take place in a highly industrialized country, does nevertheless claim to be a society of the kind which Marx predicted would follow the destruction of capitalism. It claims, that is, to be a classless society, at least in the sense that there is no hierarchy of classes and no domination by one class over others. This claim is based mainly upon the fact that the private ownership of the means of production has been abolished. Social theorists in the USSR have rarely attempted to analyse the social and political foundations of a classless society, and for long periods, especially after 1930, they were at some pains to make a sharp distinction between 'classlessness' and 'egalitarianism'. The latter was denounced as a 'petty *bourgeois* deviation', and the Soviet Encyclopaedia of Stalin's time asserted that 'socialism and egalitarianism have nothing in common'.[25] This ideological offensive against egalitarianism coincided broadly with the change in policy of the Soviet rulers in the early 1930's, which involved increasing wage and salary differentials, and in particular offering substantial financial incentives to highly skilled workers, scientists and technicians, industrial managers and intellectuals. These policies were continued during and after the war, and as a result the range of incomes in the USSR came to be almost as great as that in the capitalist countries. It is estimated that in 1953 industrial incomes ranged between 3,500–5,000 roubles a year for an unskilled worker, and 80,000–120,000 roubles for an important factory manager. The top incomes were, therefore, some 25–30 times as great as those at the bottom, which is perhaps somewhat less than the difference in Britain or the USA between the income of an unskilled worker and that of a managing director. But when the effects of taxation are considered, the income range in the USSR may have been greater, for the Soviet income tax is not steeply progressive, and taxation as a whole

[25] An English Socialist, on the other hand, has written: 'Where there is no egalitarianism there is no Socialism.' Roy Jenkins, 'Equality' in *New Fabian Essays* (1952).

is regressive, since the greater part of the budget income is derived from a turnover tax on food and textile goods of mass consumption. These inequalities of income have been enhanced by other factors; by the abolition of the progressive inheritance tax in 1943, and by the privileges accorded to the higher social strata in education and housing, in the use of special shops, the acquisition of cars and other scarce goods and the award of prizes, grants and annuities.

The policy of increasing income differentiation could be explained by the demands of rapid industrialization in the 1930's, and later by the needs of war and postwar reconstruction. This is not, I think, the whole explanation; but in so far as it contains some truth, we might infer that with the completion of the stage of rapid industrialization (which Rostow has called the 'drive to maturity') in the USSR, there would be a slackening, or even a reversal, of the trend towards greater inequality. A recent study[26] suggests that this is in fact happening. The author observes that since 1956 a number of policy statements have emphasized the raising of minimum wages, and he quotes the programme of the 22nd Congress of the CPSU to the effect that in the next 20 years 'the disparity between high and comparatively low incomes must be steadily reduced'.[27] He goes on to calculate, from Soviet statistics, which have become more abundant in recent years, that wage differentials have declined considerably since 1956; for example, whereas the average earnings of engineering technical personnel exceeded those of manual workers by two and a half times in the early 1930's, they were only 50 per cent higher in 1960. He concludes : 'The period since 1956 has been marked by a narrowing of skill differentials in wage rates, substantial increases in minimum wages, and the declining importance of the piece-rate system.'[28]

Even at the time when the inegalitarian features of Soviet society were so blatant, it was often argued that they did not signify the growth of a new class system. A sympathetic French observer of Soviet society put the argument as follows : 'Some

[26] Murray Yanowitch, 'The Soviet Income Revolution', *Slavic Review* XXIII (4), December, 1963.
[27] op. cit. p. 684.
[28] ibid. p. 692.

people might be tempted to conclude on the basis of this profound wage differentiation that Soviet society has not, in reality, abolished classes . . . It seems to me that classes as they exist in Western countries have actually no true equivalent in the USSR. The prejudices based on wealth, rigid barriers, the organized opposition of one class to its enlargement from below —these no longer exist or are in process of disappearing for ever in the Soviet Union. Widespread education, the encouragement profusely given by the authorities to the social advance of those elements which have been less well placed to start with—all this points towards a final result that may legitimately be termed a "classless society" . . . That is why, if anyone may argue about the presence or absence of classes in the USSR, one must in any case recognize that the upper classes are abundantly open to members of the lower classes, and that the privileged levels have nothing of crystallization, rigidity, or especially heredity about them.'[29]

The high rate of social mobility, and the absence of important barriers against mobility have often been adduced in this way as evidence for the gradual disappearance of social classes in the USSR. But the argument is open to several objections. In the first place, there has been no comprehensive study of social mobility in the USSR which would permit such definite assertions about its rate, either in absolute terms or in comparison with other societies.[30] Social mobility may have been considerable in the past half century, but it can be explained by the rapid industrialization of the country, and by losses in war (that is, by the same factors as in some Western countries) rather than by any distinctive features of the social structure. Industrial development created an array of new positions in the higher levels of the social hierarchy, and while the employed population doubled between 1926 and 1937, the *intel-*

[29] Michel Gordey, *Visa to Moscow* (English trans. 1962).

[30] One of the very few sources of data is the Harvard study of Soviet émigrés; see A. Inkeles and R.A. Bauer, *The Soviet Citizen: Daily Life in a Totalitarian Society* (1959). This is obviously not a study of a representative sample, but such as it is it indicates that the amount of movement from manual into non-manual occupations as a whole is not exceptionally high in the USSR when compared with some Western societies, but that movement from the manual strata into the *élites* is particularly high. (For these comparisons see S.M. Miller, op. cit.).

ligentsia (officials, professional and scientific workers, managers, and clerical workers) increased nearly four times. The increase in certain occupations was even more spectacular; the numbers of engineers and architects increased nearly eight times, and the numbers of scientific workers nearly six times.[81]

The process of expansion of white collar occupations is still continuing, but in the USSR as in other industrial countries, the rate of expansion is likely to slow down as industrial maturity is reached (if we exclude, for the present, the possible effects of automation), and the degree of mobility will come to depend more directly upon social policies designed to promote the interchange of individuals between the various social strata. In the later years of Stalin's régime, there were some indications that social mobility was being restricted, while the social privileges of the upper strata were more strongly emphasized. One step in this direction was the introduction, in 1940, of fees in higher education and in the last 3 years of secondary education. This increased the existing bias in favour of the upper strata in the selection of university students, and thus of the next generation of the *intelligentsia*. The reservation of high positions for those in the upper strata was aided by the new inheritance laws and by the strengthening of family ties.[82]

Nevertheless, the upper levels of Soviet society probably remained fairly open and accessible to talented individuals from the lower strata, and in recent years there have been attempts to deal with those influences which restrict mobility, for example in the sphere of education. Such efforts have been helped by the general movement to curb privilege and to bring about a greater equality of economic condition. Even at the time when income inequalities were increasing there were other factors which made for social equality over a large part of Soviet society. There was, and is, no real 'leisure class' in the USSR; and the fact that social status depends mainly upon occupation—that is, upon a definite contribution to the well-being of society (however arbitrarily the relative value of the contributions may be determined in some cases)—limits the social effects of economic differences. It seems clear from the

[81] See S.M. Schwartz, *Labour in the Soviet Union* (1952).

[82] See Alex Inkeles, 'Social Stratification and Mobility in the Soviet Union', *American Sociological Review*, August, 1950.

experience of Western countries that the social distinctions based upon property ownership and inheritance are more strongly felt, and are more divisive in their effects, than those which arise from differences in earned income. Again, the divisions created in the USSR by income differences were moderated by the fact that some skilled manual workers were also highly paid, while others could improve their position through activity in the party organizations; and still more by the absense of such profound social and cultural differences between manual and non-manual workers as exist in most of the Western countries.[33]

Yet in the opinion of many sociologists the facts we have been considering do not bear directly upon the most significant aspect of the class structure in Soviet society. However 'classless' social relationships may be at some levels of society, is there not, in the Soviet type of society, a governing *élite* which resembles closely the ruling classes of other societies, except that its power is more concentrated and less subject to restraint? Milovan Djilas, in *The New Class*, has argued that the Communist Party officials in these societies have come to constitute a new ruling class which, in his words, is '. . . made up of those who have special privileges and economic preference because of the administrative monopoly they hold.'[34] Similarly, S. Ossowski, in the work quoted earlier, emphasizes the extent to which in the modern world, and especially in the Soviet countries, changes in the class structure are brought about by the decisions of political authorities; or as he says later, by compulsion or force.[35] Thus classes no longer arise spontaneously from the economic activities of individuals; instead a

[33] The separation between manual workers and non-manual workers in the Western countries in leisure time activities is well established by sociological research. On France, see especially P.H. Chombart de Lauwe, *L'Agglomération Parisienne* (1952); on England, T.B. Bottomore, 'Social Stratification in Voluntary Organizations' in D.V. Glass (ed।)., *Social Mobility in Britain* (1954). Numerous studies, from R.A. and H.M. Lynd's *Middletown* (1929) to recent investigations of voluntary associations, point to the same phenomenon in the USA. This separation is beginning to break down, perhaps, with rising levels of living, but there is little evidence as yet to show any radical change.

[34] op. cit. p. 39.

[35] S. Ossowski, *Class Structure in the Social Consciousness*, pp. 184, 186.

political *élite* imposes upon society the type of stratification to be found in a bureaucratic hierarchy.

The most comprehensive expression of this view has been given by Raymond Aron in two articles published in 1950,[86] and more recently in his book *La lutte de classes*.[87] Aron asserts that the members of the ruling group in Soviet society have

'. . . infinitely more power than the political rulers in a democratic society, because both political and economic power are concentrated in their hands . . . Politicians, trade union leaders, public officials, generals and managers all belong to one party and are part of an authoritarian organization. The unified *élite* has absolute and unbounded power.'[88]

Another element in its power is the ideological monopoly which it enjoys through its control of the exposition and interpretation of an official creed—Marxism—which shapes the thoughts and opinions of the people and provides justifications for the actions of the ruling group. Aron contrasts this unified Soviet *élite* with the divided *élite*, or plurality of *élites*, in the democratic capitalist countries, and he seeks to explain the difference by the presence or absence of classes and other autonomous interest groups in the society.

These observers agree in discovering a profound division in Soviet society between the ruling *élite* and the rest of the population. Are they right in supposing that this signifies the formation of a new class system? Or is it only a temporary feature in a movement towards a genuinely classless society? Defenders of the Soviet régime have portrayed the Stalinist period—during which the privileges of the upper stratum, political dictatorship, and rule by violence, attained an extreme point—as an historical aberration, resulting from what is now termed the 'cult of personality'. But this is no explanation. The cult of personality has itself to be explained, and this is all the more necessary and urgent since its appearance contradicts

[86] Raymond Aron, 'Social Structure and the Ruling Class', *British Journal of Sociology*, I (1) March, 1950, and I (2) June, 1950.

[87] Raymond Aron, *La lutte de classes* (Paris, 1964). See especially Chapters IX and X.

[88] Article cit., *British Journal of Sociology*, I (2) p. 131.

all the expectations which Marxists had about the nature of a classless society. An explanation might be attempted by stating the social conditions which are favourable to the rise of charismatic leaders, along the lines which Max Weber first suggested. In the particular instance of the USSR we could point to such features as the sudden break with the past in the revolution, and the stresses, together with the need for authority and discipline, engendered by the rapid industrialization of an economically backward country. Or else, we may look for more general conditions which favour a unified *élite*, as Aron does when he argues that a 'classless society' (in the restricted sense of a society in which all economic enterprises are publicly owned and managed) necessarily produces a great concentration of power in the hands of the political and industrial leaders; and as Ossowski does when he suggests that political power has now become so important in all the industrial countries, but especially in the Soviet countries, that the political *élite* is able to form and change the system of stratification rather than being itself a product of that system.

These ideas are at variance with Marx's conception of the relation between property ownership, social classes, and political power; and also with his account of how the class system in modern societies would develop. The great extension of the activities of government, in economic development and in the provision of social services; the growth of highly organized and powerful political parties; the influence which can be exerted through the modern media of communication; these have all worked to establish a major division in society between the governing *élite*—which may include political and military leaders, high officials, and the directors of important economic enterprises—and the mass of the population, to some extent independently of social classes based upon property ownership, or of other forms of stratification. In the USSR where this division is most firmly established—because the political rulers belong to a party, revolutionary in origin, which has an exceptionally rigorous organization, and which is further bound together by an all-embracing ideology—it is also most profoundly obscured, because the doctrine to which the ruling *élite* adheres excludes either recognition or investigation of such a phenomenon.

At least, this has been the case until recently. Now at last some fresh life appears to be stirring in the long insensible body of orthodox Marxism; and not only are Marx's ideas and theories being re-examined in a more critical spirit, but the social structure of the Soviet countries is beginning to be studied in a more realistic and objective manner. As a result, the problems of the centralization of power are now more open to rational discussion; and the attempts to combine public ownership and central planning with the creation of relatively independent local centres of decision, such as are being made in Yugoslavia through the institutions of workers' self-management, are no longer rejected out of hand as sinister deviations from orthodoxy. The Yugoslav experience, in fact, seems to many socialists (Marxist and other) to hold out the promise of an eventual classless society in which there would be neither political dictatorship nor total intellectual conformity. At the same time it illustrates very strikingly the newly tolerated diversity of institutions and doctrines within the Soviet group of countries.

The capitalist societies, as we have seen already, are also diverse in their class structure, and any comparison between the Soviet and the capitalist forms of industrial society must recognize that there is a considerable range of variation within each type of society—for example, in the nature and extent of social mobility, in the magnitude of economic inequalities, in the situation of the working class and in the degree of unification of the *élite*—which makes for a continuum of differences rather than an abrupt break between the two types. This fact, which is unpalatable to the more extreme ideologists on both sides, is given further emphasis by the common features in Soviet and capitalist societies which result mainly from three important influences upon all modern societies : the rapid progress of industrialization, the growing size of organizations, especially in the economic sphere, and the increasing part played by governments in the deliberate shaping of economic and social life.

Industrialization has sometimes been regarded by sociologists as a process which tends naturally to bring about a greater

CLASSES IN THE INDUSTRIAL SOCIETIES

equality of condition in society. This view is supported by various arguments. The development of industry breaks down any rigid and exclusive differences of rank, by creating unprecedented opportunities for social mobility, by extending and improving education to meet the new scientific and technological needs, and by raising enormously the general level of living, thus reducing the harshness of the contrast between the conditions of the upper and lower strata of society. Furthermore, modern industry, by increasing the size of societies, as well as the amount of mobility, creates circumstances which are especially favourable to the diffusion of egalitarian ideas, as Bouglé attempted to show in a work, now much neglected, on *Les idées égalitaires*;[39] and at the same time it brings into being a large and articulate social group—the industrial workers—capable of initiating a political movement which gives a great impetus to the spread of egalitarian and democratic ideas.

This relationship between industrialization and social stratification can be seen very well in the present day developing countries. In many of them there are, or have been until recently, extremes of wealth and poverty much greater than those in the industrial countries; and the traditional upper classes have constituted a formidable obstacle to economic development, by their general resistance to change and mobility, and by their propensity to use the large share of the national income which they receive for conspicuous consumption rather than productive investment. Where industrialization gets under way successfully it is very often at the expense of upper class wealth and privileges, through confiscation or high taxation, and the opening of *élite* occupations to talented individuals from the lower social strata. Conversely, where, as in India, an extraordinarily intricate and inflexible traditional form of stratification successfully resists any radical changes, the pace of industrialization may be greatly diminished, and the whole endeavour to promote economic growth be put in jeopardy.

It would be quite wrong, however, to suppose that industrialization leads inexorably to an egalitarian society. The evidence

---

[39] C. Bouglé, *Les idées égalitaires: Étude sociologique* (Paris, 1925).

we have already considered shows that in the Western industrial societies there has been little reduction of economic inequality in the past few decades, while in the USSR inequality actually increased between the 1930's and the 1950's, to some extent as part of a policy of incentives to induce more rapid industrialization. Moreover, the other influences at work in modern societies, mentioned earlier, tend to increase social inequality, by accentuating the distinction between *élites* and masses. The increasing size and the growing rationalization of business enterprises has had this effect, by establishing a small group of top managers, supported by expert advisers, in remote control of the routine and largely unskilled activities of large numbers of workers. Other large organizations, including the modern political parties, also display some of the same features. The increasing scope and powers of the central government is another aspect of this process in which the making of important decisions tends to be more and more concentrated in a few hands, while the powers of independent voluntary associations and of local elected bodies decline.

The principal difference between the Soviet countries and the capitalist democracies is to be found in the character of the *élites*, and its political consequences, rather than in the other aspects of social stratification. As we have seen, the range of incomes in these societies is broadly similar, and everywhere large differences of income produce distinctions between social groups in their styles of life, their opportunitties and their social prestige. In the early 1950's, it appeared that economic inequalities were increasing in the Soviet societies and diminishing (though very slowly) in the capitalist societies. At the present time, both these trends seem to have been reversed, but it is difficult as yet to foresee the consequences of these changes. One fact does mark an important contrast : namely, that in the Soviet societies, economic inequalities do not arise to any significant extent from differences in wealth, whereas the distinctions between property-owners and property-less workers, between income from property, and income from work, run all through the capitalist societies, and largely account for the strong sentiments of class position which are manifest there. This circumstance is connected with the fact that the distinctions between whole social groups are less obvious and less emphasized in the Soviet societies. Income differences produce some separation of groups, but it is probably the case that social intercourse between individuals in different occupations and income levels is a great deal easier than in the capitalist countries. One of the major divisions in Soviet society has probably been that between town and country, between urban workers and peasants. How far the gap has diminished in the USSR in recent years it is difficult to determine in the absence of serious research, but studies in other countries—notably in Yugoslavia and Poland—indicate that it is still considerable; and its full extent is shown by the problems of acculturation which arise when peasants are recruited for industrial work in the course of economic development.

The contrast between the unified ruling *élite* in the Soviet countries and the divided *élite* in the capitalist democracies, which has been so much emphasized by sociologists during the past decade, has itself to be interpreted with great care if we are to escape the absurd view that in one of these types of society there is a completely monolithic ruling party, while in the other there is no ruling group at all. The Soviet societies approach more or less closely the ideal type of a unified *élite*, which suppresses any opposition, whether political or intellectual, from other social forces, as well as any conflict within its own ranks; but it is clear that these societies have experienced in practice very serious conflicts between different interest groups, and that in recent years the opportunities for such interest groups to express criticism and to influence policy have increased.

In the capitalist societies, on the other hand, the evident division of the *élite* into divergent interest groups at one level does not preclude the existence at another level of important *common* interests and aspirations which tend to produce a uniformity of outlook and action on fundamental issues of social policy. The *élites* in these societies are recruited very largely from an upper class which has its own distinctive economic and cultural interests, and their provenance is likely to shape to a common pattern, the ends and forms of action which they adopt. Even where the association between an upper class and the *élite* groups is less strong the latter may still, by virtue of the manifold connections which are established between those who wield power in various spheres, come to act generally in concert, despite the conflicts between them on particular occasions. This is the principal argument of C. Wright Mills in *The Power Elite*; but he goes further in suggesting that the development of modern society tends to produce, by the centralization of power and the elimination or weakening of local and voluntary associations, a 'mass society', the rudiments of which can be discerned everywhere, and which is gradually taking the place of the older form of industrial society with its division into social classes.[40]

However, it is not so much the homogeneity or heterogeneity of the ruling *élite* as the possibility of forming and establishing organizations which *oppose* the *élite* in power, which constitutes the principal difference between the Soviet societies and the capitalist democracies. Old-fashioned Marxists explain this disparity very easily, by observing that there are, in the Soviet societies, no exploiting or exploited classes, thus no class antagonisms, and thus no basis for political conflict; whereas in the capitalist democracies, it is precisely the existence of classes having opposed interests which engenders the major political conflicts. The second part of this statement is very generally accepted, though with many qualifications which were indicated in our earlier discussion;[41] but the first part will not bear serious examination. In many of the Soviet societies—and especially in the USSR—there have been profound social conflicts, which have erupted from time to time in large scale revolts; as for example in the resistance of the Russian peasants to collectivization in the 1930's, and in the uprising of the Hungarian people in 1956. If these conflicts have not given rise to any sustained public opposition to the ruling *élite* it is only because they have been forcibly repressed. The absence of an organized opposition is no indication at all of a state of society in which harmony and co-operation have replaced conflict when it results in this way from the persistent use of violence by the political rulers. Marx was consist-

[40] C. Wright Mills, *The Power Elite,* p. 304. '. . . we have moved a considerable distance along the road to the mass society. At the end of that road there is totalitarianism, as in Nazi Germany or in Communist Russia.'

[41] See above, pp. 21–3, 26–8.

ent in arguing, from his premises, that with the abolition of classes the major source of political conflict in society would be eliminated, and that the need for a coercive state would then disappear. In the phrase of Saint-Simon, which Marx adopted, 'the government of men is replaced by the administration of things'. It is all too evident that this is not what has happened in the Soviet societies. On the contrary the repressive apparatus of the state has grown enormously;[42] and although in the USSR and other east European countries the rule of force has been moderated since the death of Stalin, government is still much more coercive than in the capitalist societies. Of late there has been more outspoken criticism; and in some spheres which do not affect very closely the political régime, a greater freedom of thought and imagination has been permitted. The official doctrines of socialist realism in art, music and literature, seem, happily, to be expiring. But there is still neither freedom of movement for the individual, nor any possibility of organized public dissent and opposition on important questions of social policy. In certain respects, as in the introduction of the death penalty for various economic offences, the coercive power of the state has been enhanced,[43] and the existence of serious conflict within the society all the more clearly demonstrated.

Two general conclusions may be drawn from this discussion. The first is that the extent of conflict, and of coercive government, in the Soviet societies, indicates either that classes and class antagonisms have survived or have been re-created in a new form in these societies; or else that there are other important sources of social conflicts besides those of class interest, and that if, through the influence of a doctrinaire creed such

---

[42] Except in Yugoslavia, which has remained largely outside the sphere of influence of the USSR.

[43] Marx himself consistently opposed the coercive power of the state, and he expressed himself forthrightly on the subject of capital punishment, in a passage which is peculiarly apposite to the present conditions in the Soviet countries: 'Now, what a state of society is that which knows of no better instrument for its own defence than the hangman, and which proclaims . . . its own brutality as eternal law? . . . is there not a necessity for deeply reflecting upon an alteration of the system that breeds these crimes, instead of glorifying the hangman who executes a lot of criminals to make room only for the supply of new ones?' 'Capital Punishment', *New York Daily Tribune*, February 18, 1853.

conflicts are denied expression, this can only be accomplished in the last resort by violence. The second conclusion is that if the main source of political and ideological conflicts in the modern capitalist societies has been the opposition between classes, and if such conflicts have helped to establish some of the vital conditions of democracy—the right of dissent and criticism, the right to create associations independently of the state—then it must be considered whether the abolition, or even the decline of social classes does not open the way for the growth of a mass society, in which the political *élite* has unbounded power, just as much as for the creation of an egalitarian and democratic society.

IV

Social Class, Politics and Culture

The egalitarian movement which came to life in socialist clubs, trade unions, co-operative ventures, and utopian communities, grew stronger throughout the nineteenth century as capitalism developed. In the course of time this movement has taken many different forms—struggles for women's rights and against racial discrimination, and most recently the efforts to close the gap between rich and poor nations—but its driving force has remained the opposition to the hierarchy of social classes. The class system of the capitalist societies is seen as the very fount of inequality, from which arise the chief impediments to individual achievement and enjoyment, the major conflicts within and between nations, and the political dominance of privileged minorities.

In this movement Marx's analysis of capitalist society acquired—directly or indirectly—a large influence, through the connections which it established between social classes and political institutions. According to Marx, the upper class in society—constituted by the owners of the principal means of production—is necessarily the *ruling* class; that is, it also controls the means of political domination—legislation, the courts, the administration, military force, and the agencies of intellectual persuasion. The other classes in society, which suffer in various ways under this domination, are the source of political opposition, of new social doctrines, and eventually of a new ruling class. Only in the modern capitalist societies, however, does a situation occur in which the contending classes are reduced to two clearly demarcated groups, one of which—the working class—because it contains no significant new social divisions within itself, espouses an egalitarian creed and engages in a political struggle to bring about a classless society.

The appeal of Marx's theory is twofold : it provides a clear and inspiring formulation of the aspirations of the working class, and at the same time it offers an explanation of the development of forms of society and government, and especially of the rise of the modern labour movement itself. There are not lacking, in the present age, governments which are quite plainly the instruments of rule by an upper class, as in those economically backward countries where the landowners dominate an uneducated, unorganized and dispirited peasantry. When Marx undertook his studies the class character of governments was just as apparent in the European countries which had embarked upon industrialization. During much of the nineteenth century only property owners in these societies enjoyed full political rights; and it was scarcely an exaggeration to conceive the government as 'a committee for managing the common affairs of the *bourgeoisie* as a whole'. In many European countries it was only during the first two decades of the twentieth century that universal suffrage was finally established.

Since political democracy is such a recent growth Marx can hardly be blamed for having failed to consider all its implications for the association between economic and political power. At least he did not disregard the importance of the suffrage. In an article of 1852, in which he discussed the political programme of the Chartists he wrote :

'The carrying of Universal Suffrage in England would, therefore, be a far more socialistic measure than anything which has been honoured with that name on the Continent. Its inevitable result, here, is the *political supremacy of the working class*.'[1]

On a later occasion, it is true, Marx referred in a more disparaging way to the right of 'deciding once in 3 or 6 years which member of the ruling class was to misrepresent the people in Parliament'.[2] But he added immediately : 'On the

[1] Karl Marx, 'The Chartists', *New York Daily Tribune,* August 25, 1852. This article was conspicuously omitted from the first edition (1954) of the official Communist collection of Marx and Engels' writings on Britain but has been included in the new edition (1962).

[2] *The Civil War in France* (1871).

other hand, nothing could be more foreign to the spirit of the Commune than to supersede universal suffrage by hierarchic investiture.' The situations which called forth these divergent assessments were in fact very different. In the one case Marx was describing a state of affairs in which a working class movement, organized on a large scale, would be capable of putting forward its own trusted candidates at elections; while in the other he was drawing a contrast between an actual working class government—the Commune—and a preceding condition in which the working class was able to vote only for one or another of the *bourgeois* parties.

The existence of large working class parties has become a normal feature of the democratic capitalist countries, and this is one of the principal circumstances (another being the political system in the Soviet societies) which raises new problems concerning the relationship between class and politics. In a political system of this kind can the owners of property be regarded any longer as a permanent ruling class? Is the working class still a radical, revolutionary force which seeks to bring about an egalitarian society? Are the relations between classes in the political sphere still the same as they were in the nineteenth-century societies with their restricted franchise? Have new political divisions emerged alongside, or in the place of, those between classes; or have political conflicts lost some of the urgency and importance which they acquired in the period which saw the rise and growth of the labour movement? These questions lie at the heart of present controversies about the changing class structure of industrial societies.

It has become common, for example, to remark upon the great complexity of government in modern societies, and upon the influence which is exerted by the diverse interest groups which are consulted in the course of policy making; and then to argue that where power is divided among many different groups, whose interests do not always coincide, the notion of a 'ruling class' has lost all meaning. But if power is really so widely dispersed how are we to account for the fact that the owners of property—the upper class in Marx's sense—still predominate so remarkably in government and administration, and in other *élite* positions; or that there has been so little

redistribution of wealth and income, in spite of the strenuous
and sustained effort of the labour movement to bring it about?
Is it not reasonable to conclude, from the evidence provided
in the last chapter, that notwithstanding political democracy,
and despite the limited conflicts of interest which occur between *élite* groups in different spheres, the upper class in the
capitalist societies is still a distinctive and largely self-perpetu-
ating social group, and still occupies the vital positions of
power? Its power may be less commanding, and it is certainly
less arrogantly exercised, than in an earlier period, because it
encounters an organized opposition and the test of elections,
and because other classes have gained a limited access to the
élites; but the power which it has retained enables it to defend
successfully its most important economic interests.

There are other difficulties with the concept of a 'ruling
class', but I have examined them at length elsewhere[3] and I
shall not consider them further in the present context. It is in
any case the changes in the condition of the working class, and
especially in its political role, which have most impressed students of class structure in the postwar period. The 'new working
class', it is claimed, is economically prosperous and aspires
to middle class standards of living :[4] and in consequence it has
become less class conscious and less radical in politics. How far
are these political inferences warranted? Class consciousness,
in a broad sense, may be regarded as one form of the 'consciousness of kind' which develops in all enduring social groups;
for example, the consciousness of belonging to a particular
nation. In this sense, the emergence of class consciousness,
the increasing use of the term 'class' to describe an individual's position in society, is itself a sign that new social
groups have come into existence.[5] But in Marx's usage, which
has had a profound influence both upon sociological theories
and upon political doctrines, 'class consciousness' involves
something more than this; namely, the gradual formation of
distinctive ideologies and political organizations which have

[3] See my *Elites and Society*. Chapter II.
[4] See above, pp. 28–30.
[5] There is a good account by Asa Briggs, 'The Language of "Class" in
Early Nineteenth Century England' in Asa Briggs and John Saville (eds.),
Essays in Labour History (1960).

as their object the promotion of particular class interests in a general conflict between classes.[6]

The growing class consciousness of the working class was represented by Marx as showing these characteristics in an exceptional degree; for it was expressed in ideologies and political movements which strongly emphasized the conflict of economic interest between capitalists and workers, and which proposed radical social changes in order to end the system of society based upon classes. The working class was, therefore, a revolutionary element in society; more revolutionary indeed than any earlier oppressed classes, since it aimed consciously at abolishing the whole class system. As Marx wrote, with youthful enthusiasm, in a sketch of his theory of modern classes which guided all his mature thinking :

'A class must be formed which has *radical chains*, a class *in* civil society which is not a class *of* civil society, a class which is the dissolution of all classes, a sphere of society which has a universal character because its sufferings are universal, and which does not claim a *particular redress* because the wrong which is done to it is not a *particular wrong* but *wrong in general*. There must be formed a sphere of society which claims no *traditional* status but only a *human* status . . . a sphere finally which cannot emancipate itself without emancipating itself from all the other spheres of society, without therefore emancipating all these other spheres; which is, in short, a *total loss* of humanity and which can only redeem itself by a *total redemption of humanity*. This dissolution of society, as a particular class, is the proletariat.'[7]

This conception of the working class as the animator of a revolutionary movement which is to establish a classless society, appears to many sociologists to be highly questionable in the light of recent investigations. It is not that the prevalence of

[6] Writing about the peasantry in *The Eighteenth Brumaire of Louis Bonaparte* Marx observed: 'In so far as there is merely a local interconnection among these smallholding peasants, and the identity of their interests begets no community, no national bond, and no political organization among them, they do not form a class.'

[7] Karl Marx, 'Critique of Hegel's Philosophy of Right', in *Deutsch-Französische Jahrbücher* (1844).

class consciousness in a broad sense, or the association between class membership and political affiliation, is generally
denied. Social surveys have shown plainly that most people
are familiar with the class structure of their society, and are
aware of their own position within it. Equally, it has been
shown that class membership is still the strongest single influence upon a person's social and political attitudes; and that
the major political parties in most countries represent pre-
eminently class interests. What is brought into question by
recent studies is the view that the working class, in the advanced
industrial countries, is striving to bring about a revolutionary
transformation of society, rather than piecemeal reforms within the existing social structure; or that there is a total incompatibility and opposition between the doctrines and objectives
of political parties which draw their main support from different classes. In Marx's theory the working class was revolutionary in two senses : first, that it aimed, or would aim, to produce
the most comprehensive and fundamental change in social
institutions that had ever been accomplished in the history of
mankind, and secondly, that it would do so in the course of a
sustained conflict with the *bourgeoisie* which was likely to culminate in a violent struggle for power. The nascent working
class of the mid-nineteenth century fitted reasonably well into
this scheme, which was constructed largely out of the experiences of the French revolution. The 'new working class' of the
mid-twentieth century, it is argued, fits badly.

Studies of industrial workers during the past decade agree
broadly in finding that there has been a decline in their attach-
ment to collective ends, and so also in their enthusiasm for
action as a class in order to establish a new social order. F.
Zweig, in his study of workers in four modern enterprises, observes that 'when speaking about classes a man would seem to
be thinking primarily about himself, about the individual aspect of the problem, and not about the social situation or the
social structure',[8] and he goes on to say that although two-
thirds of the workers he interviewed placed themselves in the
working class, this recognition of their *class identity* was not
accompanied by any strong feelings of *class allegiance*. A study

[8] F. Zweig. *The Worker in an Affluent Society* (1961) p. 134.

of French workers[9] arrives at very similar conclusions. The authors distinguish three types of reaction among factory workers to their situation in the economy and in society : (1) evasion (the attempt to escape from industrial work either by rising to a higher position within the firm or by setting up in business on one's own account); (2) resignation (a dull and resentful acceptance of industrial work as an inescapable fate); and (3) revolt (opposition and resistance to the capitalist organization of industry). Of these three types, the second is by far the most common, while the third is the least so; and even the 9 per cent of workers in this category, who believe that they can improve their situation by collective action, no longer believe that any future society will be able to alter fundamentally the subordinate position of the worker in the factory. The authors summarize their results by saying that although the workers they studied still have a group conscious-ness (i.e. they regard themselves as 'workers', clearly distin-guished from other groups in the population), they no longer have any collective aims. The present-day worker is 'a man who is cut off from working class traditions and who possesses no general principles, no world-view, which might give a direc-tion to his life'.[10] This conclusion, they observe, agrees entirely with those reached in a number of studies in Germany, by Popitz, Bednarik and others. Popitz and his collaborators, in their study of workers in the Ruhr steel industry,[11] show that there is a strong working class consciousness, which is built around the distinction between manual workers and those who plan, direct and command work; but those who still think in Marxist terms of the victory of the working class and the attain-ment of a classless society are a small minority. Similarly, Bed-narik concludes his essay on the young worker of today by saying that 'society has ceased to be an ideal for the working class', and that the worker 'tends more and more to withdraw into private life'.[12]

[9] A. Andrieux, J. Lignon, *L'Ouvrier d'aujourd, hui* (1960).

[10] op. cit. p. 189.

[11] H. Popitz, H.P. Bahrdt, E.A. Jüres, H. Kesting, *Das Gesellschaftsbild des Arbeiters* (1957).

[12] K. Bednarik, *Der junge Arbeiter von heute—ein neuer Typ* (1953), pp. 138-9, 141.

Several of these ideas are brought together by Goldthorpe and Lockwood, in their analysis of the notion of *embourgeoisement*,[18] where it is suggested that there has been, in the Western industrial countries, a convergence between the 'new middle class' and the 'new working class', leading to a distinctive view of society which diverges both from the radical individualism of the old middle classes and from the comprehensive collectivism of the old working class. In this new social perspective collectivism is widely accepted as a means (and this accounts for the spread of trade unionism among white collar workers), but no longer as an end (which accounts for the weakening of class allegiance among workers). Goldthorpe and Lockwood use the terms 'instrumental collectivism' and 'family centredness' to describe the complex of beliefs and attitudes in this conception of society. The second term refers to the phenomenon which other writers have described as a withdrawal into private life, and which is revealed by the individual worker's predominant concern with his family's standard of living, his own prospects of advancement, the education of his children and their opportunities to enter superior occupations.

The second feature of the working class as a revolutionary force, namely its involvement in violent class struggles, can be discussed more briefly. In all the advanced industrial countries the violence of class conflict has greatly diminished over the past few decades, and the working class parties which still regard their aims as likely to be achieved by the use of force are few in number and insignificant. The change from the conditions at the end of the nineteenth century has been produced by several factors, among which we may single out the development of political democracy, the more effective power of modern governments, aided by the great advances in military technology, in administration and in communication, and the changes in the nature of working class aims as well as in the relations between classes. It would be a mistake to dismiss entirely the role of force in political conflicts in the Western industrial societies; for not only did violent class struggles take place as recently as the 1930's, but other types of social conflict —for example, between Negroes and whites in the USA—have

[18] John H. Goldthorpe, David Lockwood, 'Affluence and the British Class Structure', *Sociological Review*, XI (2) July, 1963. See above, pp. 29–30.

often engendered violence during the past decade. Nevertheless, at the present time it is in those countries which have just embarked upon industrialization that violent struggles, especially between classes, are mainly to be found.

Changes in the relations between classes in the capitalist societies have accompanied the changes in the character of the major social classes, influencing and being influenced by the latter. In so far as social mobility has increased, and the middle class has grown in numbers, the image of society as divided between two great contending classes has become blurred by the superimposition of another image, in which society appears as an indefinite and changing hierarchy of status positions, which merge into each other, and between which individuals and families are able to move with much greater facility than in the past. In addition, the everyday economic struggle between workers and employers has been regulated more and more by the state, through the creation of new social institutions for negotiation, arbitration and joint consultation. It is this situation which leads Ralf Dahrendorf, in his *Class and Class Conflict in Industrial Society*, to write of 'post-capitalist societies' in which industrial conflicts have been institutionalized and thereby insulated from the sphere of politics; and although this is an exaggeration, inasmuch as political conflicts are still very largely about class interests, and are widely recognized as such, it contains an element of truth in so far as it points to the moderation of hostility between classes and to the emergence of political issues which are in some measure detached from questions of class interest. There is unquestionably some common ground between the main political parties in the Western industrial countries; and the development of science and technology, economic growth and rising levels of living, urban congestion and crime, are among the issues which have to be dealt with politically along much the same lines in *all* the industrial countries.

The social changes which have produced the 'new working class', as well as a political climate in which violent confrontations between the classes are rare, have been interpreted by some sociologists as a crucial phase in a process which is leading to the complete assimilation of the working class into existing society, as a beginning of the 'end of ideology' in the precise sense of the decline of socialist doctrines which offer a radical criticism of present day society and the hope of an alternative form of society. But this interpretation goes beyond the facts which have been discovered by sociological research. It relies, for instance, upon a tacit comparison between the present state of working class consciousness and its state in some vaguely located and imperfectly known past age, which is seen as a time of heroic resolution and militancy. Against this it should be observed that in the past few decades, in the very period in which the working class is supposed to have become more middle class in its outlook, the support for socialist parties in Europe has been maintained or has substantially increased. It may be objected that this support has been gained by the progressive elimination of distinctively socialist ideas from the programmes of such parties. But this too is doubtful. The language of socialism has changed over the past century, in ways which it would be rewarding to study more closely, but the ends of the labour movement—collectivism and social equality—have not been abandoned or even seriously questioned.

The picture of working class apathy and lack of enthusiasm for collective ends which is given by the studies mentioned earlier, has to be seen, therefore, as a portrait taken at one moment of time and not as the final episode of a serial film. Even as a momentary picture it may not do justice to all the features of the situation. Serge Mallet, in his study of the 'new working class' referred to above,[14] suggests that because the worker as a producer is still dominated and constrained, while as a consumer he experiences a new freedom and independence, it is in relation to the working environment that class consciousness is most vigorously expressed;[15] and this is apparent, he thinks, in the changing nature of trade union de-

[14] Pp. 30–31 above.

[15] This appears very clearly in the comments of workers reported in the study by Andrieux and Lignon (op. cit.). They mention frequently and bitterly the difference in the treatment which they receive from other people according to whether they are recognized as workers (in the factory, travelling to work) or as citizens (in leisure time). One worker summed it up by saying that as a worker he was pushed around, but '. . . when I am out in my car and stop to ask for directions the policeman comes up touching his cap because he thinks he is dealing with a gentleman.' (pp. 31–32).

mands in the modern sectors of industry, which are concerned increasingly with shorter hours of work, longer holidays, and greater control over the policies of management. These demands reflect the desire of the 'new working class' to alter radically its position in the system of production, in a sense which is close to the ideas of classical socialist thought. The same aspirations, it may be added, find expression in the widening discussion of various forms of producers' co-operation, which has been inspired very largely by the progress of workers' self-management in Yugoslavia.

There are several other influences at work in the Western industrial societies which sustain the ideological controversies over the future form of society, and which lend support, in particular, to the socialist doctrines of the working class. One of the most important is the extension, and the more general acceptance, of public ownership of industry, public management of the economy, and public provision of a wide range of social and cultural services. The contrast between 'private opulence' and 'public squalor', to which J.K. Galbraith has pointed, has awakened many people to the fact that in modern societies many of the most valuable private amenities can only be got or preserved through public action. Individuals may be prosperous enough to provide adequately for their personal needs in food, housing, transport, and some kinds of entertainment, but they cannot individually assure what is needed for full enjoyment in the way of roads, facilities for sport and recreation, good working conditions, or a congenial and attractive urban environment. The unrestricted pursuit of private wealth and private enjoyment leads, indeed, to the impoverishment of these vital public services.

In the economic sphere the growth in the size of firms in major branches of industry, and the approach to monopolistic control in some sectors, has reduced the difference between the operations of publicly owned and privately owned enterprises; and if there is, at the present time, no great public excitement over the issue of 'nationalization' of industry this is in part because it is taken for granted that a change of ownership would not affect the economic performance of the industry. In part, also, it is due to recognition of the fact that the economy as a whole, in a modern society, must anyway be increasingly regulated and directed by the political authorities if a consistently high rate of growth is to be achieved, through the systematic application of science to production. Today the *entrepreneur* has become much less important; while the trained manager (who can perfectly well be a public servant), and the scientist have become much more important.

The increasing provision of social services by the state, which in recent times has been largely brought about by the pressure of the labour movement, has also fortified the socialist conception of a more equal, more collectivist society. Social legislation in the Welfare State may not be preponderantly egalitarian, either in intention or in effect,[16] but as it is extended and comes eventually to include an 'incomes policy' so it approaches the conditions in which, as a German social scientist has observed the task of social policy is to determine the order of priority of claims against the national product.[17] And these are conditions which would accord most fully with the institutions of a classless society.

This discussion of classes and ideologies in the Western societies, if it suggests that the working class may still be considered an independent force in poltical life, and one which still aims to bring about radical changes in the social structure, also indicates that the development of the working class has diverged in many respects from the course which Marx and the early Marxists expected it to follow. Marx's theory dealt, necessarily, with the first stages in the formation of the working class, and it proposed broad hypotheses rather than settled conclusions based upon intensive research. The Marxist sociologists—in any case few in number—have not greatly advanced the empirical study of social classes. Often they have seemed to be writing about an imaginary society, in which a pure class struggle continues inexorably, unsullied by such events of practical life as the advent of political democracy, the extension of welfare services, the growth of national income, or the increasing governmental regulation of the economy. Marx himself, through his dramatic vision of a revolutionary confrontation between the classes and his initial optimism about

[16] For a discussion of this point see T.H. Marshall, *Social Policy* (1965), Chapter 13, 'Retrospect and Prospect'.
[17] Quoted by T.H. Marshall, op. cit. p. 183.

the growth of the labour movement, gave some encouragement to an outlook of this kind. There had been *bourgeois*
revolutions, therefore there would be proletarian revolutions.

Neither Marx nor his followers examined sufficiently the
strengths and weaknesses of the major social classes in capitalist
society, many of which, indeed, have only become apparent
through the experiences of the past 50 or 60 years. Marx insisted that the ruling ideas in any society are the ideas of the
ruling class. But he did not seriously consider how important
the ideas themselves might be in sustaining that rule, or how
difficult it would be for the working class to oppose them with
its own ideas.[18] Doubtless he thought that his own social theory
would have a great effect (as it has), and he also counted upon
the economic failure of capitalism—the ever-worsening crises
—to discredit *bourgeois* ideas. In fact, *bourgeois* ideas have
only been discredited, for brief periods, in those societies which
have suffered defeat in war, and it is in such circumstances that
the major revolutions of the twentieth century have occurred.
Otherwise it is true to say that the working class in all countries
has continued to be profoundly influenced by the dominant
ideas of capitalist society; for example, by nationalism and imperialism, by the competitive, acquisitive and possessive conception of human nature and social relations, and in recent
times by a view of the overriding purpose of society as being
the creation of ever greater material wealth. The attempts to
combat these ideas reveal the immense difficulties involved in
doing so. The ideal of working class internationalism, in opposition to national rivalries and war between nations, has never
been realized in more than a fragmentary form, in the face of
differences of language and culture, and the manifold problems of establishing international associations at any level. On
the other side, the idea of competition and of activity as mainly
acquisitive easily becomes acceptable when it is associated with
equality of opportunity—real or supposed—for which the

---

[18] Among later Marxists Gramsci was the only one who gave much
serious attention to these questions, and I should think that he was influenced in this direction by the work of his compatriot Mosca, who had
introduced the term 'political formula' to describe the body of doctrine
which every ruling class, in his view, has to develop and to get accepted
by the rest of society if it is to retain power.

working class itself has striven; while the idea of uninterrupted economic growth must clearly appeal, with reason, to those who are struggling to escape from cramping poverty.

Yet in spite of these difficulties egalitarian and collectivist ideas have spread widely during this century. They have done so more slowly than Marx expected, but this might mean no more than that he made a mistake over the time scale while still being right about the general direction of change. The question now is whether these ideas have lost their vigour and have begun to recede, or whether they are still active and effective. A number of sociologists, as we have seen, observe a decline in the enthusiasm of the working class for collective ends, a loss of interest in any social mission, and the gradual erosion of a distinctive working class culture. A few, among them S.M. Lipset, regard the combination of political democracy and high levels of living as the final achievement of the 'good society', and thus as the terminal point of the labour movement : '. . . democracy is not only or even primarily a means through which different groups can attain their ends or seek the good society; it is the good society itself in operation.'[19] Lipset concedes that there is still a class struggle of sorts in the capitalist countries, but he sees it as being concerned only with the distribution of income, not with any profound changes in the social structure of culture; and he assumes that there is a constant trend towards greater equality of income which is turning the struggle into a process of limited bargaining between interest groups, while denuding it of all ideological or political significance.

There are several reasons to be cautious about accepting this view that the relative peace on the ideological front, and the apparent decline in the vigour of working class social ideals, have become permanent features of the capitalist societies; that the final form of industrial society has been reached. First, it is likely that there will be growing discontent as it becomes evident that there is no general trend towards greater economic equality, and that, on the contrary, there are very powerful movements which tend to produce a more unequal distribution of income and wealth whenever the industrial and

[19] S.M. Lipset, *Political Man*, p. 403.

political pressure of the working class is relaxed. It is obvious, for example, that in some Western countries there is a great disproportion between the modest wage increases which many industrial workers have claimed in recent years, and the large increases of salary which some groups of professional workers have demanded. Those in the professions have many advantages in pressing their claims, especially where the supply of qualified people is limited by the nature of the educational system; their actions are usually interpreted more sympathetically by the mass media than are the similar actions of industrial workers; and their class consciousness and determination to maintain or improve their established position in society appear to be waxing rather than waning. In society as a whole it is likely that the continued economic growth, which has benefited the working class, has brought even greater gains to those whose incomes are derived wholly or mainly from the ownership of capital. If, therefore, a tranquil and moderate struggle between classes or sectional interests, and ideological peace, depend upon a settled trend towards greater economic equality, they cannot be regarded at present as in any way assured.

A second consideration, which seems to me still more important, is that there is a growing discrepancy between the condition of the working class at work and in leisure time. Security of employment and rising levels of living have brought greater freedom of choice and independence of action for industrial workers outside the workplace, and younger workers in particular have taken advantage of their new opportunities. But one result of this is that the contrast between work and leisure has become more intense : at work there is still constraint, strict subordination, lack of responsibility, absence of means for self-expression. All the studies of the modern working class which I reviewed earlier bring out clearly that workers are profoundly aware of this division in their lives, and that they have a deep hatred of the present system of industrial work. They would undoubtedly recognize their condition in Marx's observation that a worker '. . . does not fulfil himself in his work but denies himself, has a feeling of misery rather than well-being, does not develop freely his mental and physical powers but is physically exhausted and mentally debased,' that '. . . his work is not voluntary but imposed, *forced labour*,' and that he '. . . feels himself at home only in his leisure time.'[20]

It is hard to believe that such a division can continue unchanged, but it may be overcome or mitigated in several different ways. Sustained economic growth may result in such a reduction of working hours and expansion of leisure time that the hierarchical and authoritarian structure of industry comes to play a negligible part in the individual's personal and social life, and is no longer a matter for concern. Or, on the other hand, there may be renewed efforts to introduce into the sphere of economic production some of the freedom and independence which exist in leisure time, and these efforts may be helped by changes in the character of production itself, as it becomes increasingly a scientific activity—using both the natural and the social sciences—which needs the services of highly educated and responsible individuals to carry it on. Most probably, there will be some combination of these two movements; but in so far as the second one takes place at all it will be through the actions of working class organizations seeking to control the labour process, which still appears, as it did to Marx, as the fundamental activity in every social system.

The rise of the working class in modern societies has been a more protracted affair than Marx supposed, and it has only rarely approached that state of decisive struggle with the *bourgeoisie* which he expected. In the future a similar gradual development appears most likely, but the end may still be Marx's ideal society, a classless society. Indeed, it is only now, when the tremendous development of the sciences has created the possibility of truly wealthy societies—but for the uncertainties of population growth and nuclear warfare—that the economic foundations of a classless society can be regarded as assured. What kinds of inequality would remain in the absence of social classes, and in conditions where individuals had independence and responsibility both at work and in leisure, can only be conjectured. There would doubtless be some differences in the prestige of occupations, in incomes, and in the social position of individuals, but there is no reason to suppose that these would be very large, or that they would be incom-

[20] Karl Marx, *Economic and Philosophical Manuscripts.*

patible with an awareness of basic human equality and community.

The principal fault in many recent studies of social classes has been that they lack an historical sense. Like the economists of whom Marx said that they believed there had been history, because feudalism had disappeared, but there was no longer any history, because capitalism was a natural and eternal social order, some sociologists have accepted that there was an historical development of classes and of class conflicts in the early period of industrial capitalism, but that this has ceased in the fully evolved industrial societies in which the working class has escaped from poverty and has attained industrial and political citizenship. But this assumption is made without any real study of the evolution of social classes in recent times, or of the social movements at the present time which reveal the possibilities of future social change. An historical analysis of the changing class structure in modern societies, such as I have merely outlined here, remains one of the most important unfulfilled tasks of sociology today.

SELECTED BIBLIOGRAPHY

General Works

ARON, RAYMOND, *La lutte de classes* (Paris, Gallimard, 1964).

DAHRENDORF, RALF, *Class and Class Conflict in Industrial Society* (London, Routledge and Kegan Paul, 1959).

DJILAS, M. *The New Class* (London, Thames and Hudson, 1957).

GEIGER, THEODOR, *Die Klassengesellschaft im Schmelztiegel* (Köln-Hagen, 1949).

INTERNATIONAL SOCIOLOGICAL ASSOCIATION, *Transactions of the Third World Congress of Sociology* (London, 1956). Vol. III.

MARSHALL, T.H., *Sociology at the Crossroads and Other Essays* (London, Heinemann, 1963). Part Two, 'Social Class'.

OSSOWSKI, S. *Class Structure in the Social Consciousness* (London, Routledge and Kegan Paul, 1963).

SCHUMPETER, J.A., 'Social Classes in an Ethnically Homogeneous Environment' in *Imperialism and Social Classes* (Oxford, Basil Blackwell, 1951).

WEBER, MAX, 'Class, Status, Party', in H.H. Gerth and C. Wright Mills (eds.) *From Max Weber: Essays in Sociology* (London, Kegan Paul, 1947), pp. 180–95.

The Upper Class

ARON, RAYMOND, 'Classe sociale, classe politique, classe dirigeante', *European Journal of Sociology*, I (2), 1960, pp. 260–82.

BALTZELL, E. DIGBY, *An American Business Aristocracy* (New York, Collier Books, 1962).

BOTTOMORE, T.B., *Elites and Society* (London, C.A. Watts and Co., 1964), Chapter II.

GUTTSMAN, W.L., *The British Political Elite* (London, MacGibbon and Kee, 1963).

MEISEL, JAMES H., *The Myth of the Ruling Class: Gaetano Mosca and the Elite* (Ann Arbor, University of Michigan Press, 1958).

MILLS, C. WRIGHT, *The Power Elite* (New York, Oxford University Press, 1956).

MOSCA, GAETANO, *The Ruling Class* (New York, McGraw-Hill, 1939).
VEBLEN, THORSTEIN, *The Theory of the Leisure Class* (1899; new edition, New York, Mentor Books, 1953, with an introduction by C. Wright Mills).

The Middle Classes

CRONER, FRITZ, *Soziologie der Angestellten* (Köln, Berlin, Kiepenheuer and Witsch, 1962).
CROZIER, MICHEL, 'Classes sans conscience ou préfiguration de la société sans classes', *European Journal of Sociology*, I (2), 1960, pp. 233–47.
Inventaires III. Classes moyennes (Paris, Félix Alcan, 1939).
LOCKWOOD, D., *The Blackcoated Worker* (London, Allen and Unwin, 1958).
MILLS, C. WRIGHT, *White Collar: The American Middle Classes* (New York, Oxford University Press, 1951).

The Working Class

ANDRIEUX, A., and LIGNON, J., *L'ouvrier d'aujourd'hui* (Paris, Marcel Rivière, 1960).
BLAUNER, R., *Alienation and Freedom: The Factory Worker and His Industry* (Chicago, University of Chicago Press, 1964).
BRIEFS, G.A., *The Proletariat* (New York, McGraw-Hill, 1937).
GOLDTHORPE, J.H., and LOCKWOOD, D., 'Affluence and the British Class Structure', *The Sociological Review*, XI (2) July, 1963, pp. 133–63.
HOGGART, R., *The Uses of Literacy* (London, Chatto and Windus, 1957).
LOCKWOOD, D., 'The "New Working Class"', *European Journal of Sociology*, I (2), 1960, pp. 248–59.
MALLET, SERGE, *La nouvelle classe ouvrière* (Paris, Editions du Seuil, 1963).
POPITZ, H., BAHRDT, H.P., JÜRES, E.A., and KESTING, H., *Das Gesellschaftsbild des Arbeiters* (Tübingen, J.C.B., Mohr, 1957).
THOMPSON, E.P., *The Making of the English Working Class* (London, Gollancz, 1964).
ZWEIG, F., *The Worker in an Affluent Society* (London, Heinemann, 1961).

Class Consciousness

HALBWACHS, M., *The Psychology of Social Class* (London, Heinemann, 1958).
CENTERS, R., *The Psychology of Social Classes* (Princeton, Princeton University Press, 1949).

LUKÀCS, G., *Geschichte und Klassenbewusstsein* (Berlin, Malik Verlag, 1923). French translation, *Histoire et conscience de classe* (Paris, Editions de Minuit, 1960).

MANNHEIM, KARL, 'Conservative Thought', in *Essays on Sociology and Social Psychology* (London, Routledge and Kegan Paul, 1953).

See also, G.A. Briefs, op. cit., Chapter VI 'The proletarian consciousness'.

Class Conflict, Social Revolution

ARENDT, HANNAH, *On Revolution* (London, Faber and Faber, 1963).

DAHRENDORF, RALF, 'Über einige Probleme der soziologischen Theorie der Revolution', *European Journal of Sociology*, II (1), 1961, pp. 153–62.

GEIGER, THEODOR, *Die Masse und ihre Aktion: ein Beitrag zur Soziologie der Revolution* (Stuttgart, 1926).

GEIGER, THEODOR, 'Revolution', in A. Vierkandt (ed.), *Handwörterbuch der Soziologie* (Stuttgart, 1931), pp. 511–18.

KAUTSKY, KARL, *The Social Revolution* (London, 1908).

MEUSEL, A., 'Revolution and Counter-revolution', in *Encyclopaedia of the Social Sciences* (New York, Macmillan, 1934), Vol. 13, pp. 367–76.

SOREL, G., *Reflections on Violence* (New edn. Glencoe, The Free Press, 1950).

See also the books by Aron and Dahrendorf mentioned under 'General Works' above.

Social Mobility

CARLSSON, G., *Social Mobility and Class Structure* (Lund, Gleerup, 1958).

FLOUD, J.E., HALSEY, A.H., and MARTIN, F.M., *Social Class and Educational Opportunity* (London, Heinemann, 1956).

GIRARD, ALAIN, *La réussite sociale en France* (Paris, Presses Universitaires de France, 1961).

GLASS, D.V., (ed.), *Social Mobility in Britain* (London, Routledge and Kegan Paul, 1954).

LIPSET, S.M., and BENDIX, R., *Social Mobility in Industrial Society* (Berkeley, University of California Press, 1959).

MILLER, S.M., 'Comparative Social Mobility', *Current Sociology*, IX (1), 1960.

SOROKIN, P.A., *Social Mobility* (New York, 1927, Reprinted with a chapter from his *Social and Cultural Dynamics*, Glencoe, The Free Press, 1959).

Index